POSSESS

Marie Tuhart

https://www.marietuhart.com/

Thank you!

POSSESS

Wicked Sanctuary: Surrender your inhibitions.

Growing up, Allyson Young learned firsthand that, sometimes, the people who are supposed to love you don't. Meaningful relationships are an illusion. Working alongside hard-to-ignore contractor Zeke Riggs causes her to rethink that love is possible.

Having been shot down twice already, Zeke asks Allyson out one more time. When she accepts, he's floored and determined to show her he's not like the other men who walked away. Breaking through Allyson's tough veneer won't be easy, but he's not letting go this time. He intends to show her how worthy she is of being cherished and loved.

Until a meal with Zeke's family drives home to Allyson she can't outrun her past and how unlovable she is. Leaving Zeke before she destroys him is the only option. Zeke must find her before everything they've built is destroyed.

ACKNOWLEGMENTS

There are several people I want to thank for supporting me through this book:

Laurie, thank you for keeping me sane while writing this book.

Isabel, for our Saturday sprint sessions and talking through issues.

Susannah, for our weekday sprint sessions and letting me vent.

Nia, for giving me great feedback on the book.
Red Quill Editing team, you are the best team to work with. You helped me shape the complex character of Allyson.

Publisher's Note: This book contains a dominant male, spunky heroine, sexy situations, and mentions of childhood trauma.

To My Readers:

This book contains elements of the BDSM lifestyle that are only true to life in this book. There are various relationship dynamics in the lifestyle, which are decided between the people involved. While I have researched and talked with people in the lifestyle, this is my take on how my characters choose to live.

If you decide to explore the lifestyle yourself, please remember to always be safe. Never go home with someone you don't know. Attend a munch or a small get-together first to see if this is something you want in your life. Reading and living are very different.

There is no mention of the coronavirus that exists in our world right now. I purposely left it out. This is a place for you to escape.
Enjoy.

Chapter 1

"You have to come with me," Dani begged Allyson.

Allyson Young regarded her friend. "Why?" Allyson turned away so her friend wouldn't see her grin.

"Please."

Allyson stifled her laughter. Dani could make one word sound like ten. "A new bookstore, you say?" Allyson worked as a building inspector for the city, and she hadn't heard anything about a new bookstore. Since jobs were assigned, her co-worker probably got it.

"Well, sort of."

Allyson turned to face her friend. "Explain, please."

"It's the expansion to Kleinman's."

"The adult store?" Allyson vaguely remembered something about it. Rudy, her co-worker, made some snide remark about being assigned to it instead of her. Especially since the construction had been done by Riggs Construction.

"Yes. They had a small book area and have monthly book club meetings, but since the book club meetings exploded, Damon decided to expand the shop."

"What do they have book club meetings about?" Allyson was curious.

"Mainly romance books. The spicy, sexy ones."

Allyson laughed. Dani loved those books. Allyson had read a few herself and liked them. "I see. Do I need to change?" She indicated her jeans and black knit shirt with puffy sleeves.

"It's perfect." Dani gave her a hug.

"Thank you for coming with me," Dani said once they were in Dani's small compact car driving toward the store.

"Sure. I don't understand why you needed me to come with you." Dani went silent, and Allyson glanced over at her. Dani's features were tight, her lips pressed together, and her fingers clenched the steering wheel. "What's going on?"

Dani stopped at a red light and looked at Allyson. "Remember when I told you I dated a guy in college?"

"Yeah, but you never told me who it was." Dani had gone to the University of Washington and studied horticulture and landscaping. Allyson stayed and went to a community college in Pleasant Valley to study urban planning and development. "You left right after you graduated to intern with a company in San Francisco."

"Right, and I came back when Gramps got sick last year." The light turned green. "Well, my college ex is going to be there."

"Oh? Do I know him?"

"You might. He works for Riggs Construction."

"It's not the owner, is it?" Allyson liked Zeke. His brown eyes would dance when he smiled and all those muscles…she wanted to run her hands over them. She and Zeke had been dancing around each other for months. Every time she thought about him, her body would go from zero to hot and bothered in about six seconds.

"No, it's not Zeke," Dani said.

Allyson breathed a sigh of relief. She could fall fast with Zeke, but she wasn't sure if she was ready to leap head first into a new relationship after her last one crashed and burned, the latest in a string of failed relationships. "Wait a second. You've been back for almost a year, and you haven't seen him?"

"No." Dani's cheeks turned red. "I've been avoiding him."

"Why?" That wasn't like her friend.

"It's complicated." Dani pulled into the almost full parking lot. "Wow, looks like there's a lot of people here."

"It's their grand opening?"

"Kind of." Dani found a spot and parked.

"What do you mean?" Her friend was holding something back.

"It was by invitation only."

"So, I'm crashing?"

"No," Dani answered. "I'm allowed to bring someone. You're my plus one."

Allyson blew out a breath. "Okay. Why didn't you RSVP in the negative?"

"Because I was expected to attend." Dani waved

her hands in the air. "Again, it's complicated." She blew out a breath. "Look, if you'd rather not come inside, I get it."

"No, it's not that." It wasn't. She'd support Dani in any way she needed. "I'm wondering why you're being so secretive about it?"

"I don't mean to be, but I did some landscaping work for Damon at his home, so he invited me, and I feel obligated to go."

"And your ex-college lover is going to be there?"

"Yep." Dani dropped her forehead to the steering wheel. "This was a bad idea."

"It's okay." Allyson put her hand on Dani's shoulder. "We go in, we mingle, and after an hour, we leave."

"Thank you." They got out of the car.

Allyson wasn't sure what she expected, but the storefront was tastefully decorated with balloons and steamers. She walked in behind Dani.

"Dani, glad you could make it." A dark-haired man hugged Dani with a smile.

"Hey, Damon. I didn't want to miss it. This is my friend, Allyson."

"Well, hello there." He took her hand and kissed the back of it. "Aren't you a delicious morsel."

Allyson frowned.

"Damon, behave." A woman with light brown hair joined them. Her voice held laughter as she slapped him on the arm. "Excuse him. He's a flirt. Hi, I'm Tessa." She held out her hand.

Damon sighed and released Allyson's hand.

"Allyson, Dani's friend."

"Well, any friend of Dani's is one of ours. Please feel free to look around. The finger food and drinks are over there." Tessa pointed to where a group of people milled around.

"Thanks, Tessa." Dani took Allyson by the arm and led her away from the couple.

"So he owns the place?" Allyson asked.

"Yes. Tessa's his girlfriend. I don't think they've gotten engaged yet."

"Then why was he flirting with me?" She frowned. That wasn't very nice of Damon.

"That's Damon. Trust me; he wouldn't do a thing to hurt Tessa."

"Hmmm."

"Allyson."

She turned at the sound of her name.

"Hi, Zeke." What was he doing there? Well, he did do the work so it would make sense he was at the opening. He looked delicious in the perfect fitting jeans and the tight black T-shirt.

"Hey, Zeke," Dani said.

"Dani." His gaze went from Dani to Allyson. "You two friends?"

"Yes," Dani glanced across the room. "Oh, I see Lara. I wanted to chat with her."

"I understand you did the remodel," she remarked, trying to stay calm. Dani walked away, seemingly without a second thought, and Allyson looked up at Zeke.

"Yep. I did." He grinned. "I'm sorry you weren't

assigned the job. Your co-worker can be a pain."

Allyson grimaced. "I want to say I'm sorry, but I don't have control over him." Why Rudy made such snide remarks about this place, she didn't know. It looked like a typical bookstore to her.

"I know. Shall we?" He held out his arm.

Manners. She'd almost forgotten men had them. "Thank you." She slipped her arm through his. It was nice to be treated like a woman instead of another guy.

"Do you want something to eat or drink? Or would you rather have a tour of the bookstore?"

"Are you playing guide?" She fluttered her lashes at him, wondering where this vixen inside her had come from. Hadn't she convinced herself this wouldn't go well?

Zeke laughed. "I'm offering my services, yes." He leaned down. "More than just a tour guide, if you're interested."

Allyson started to pull back to berate him but stopped herself. She wanted to know more about Zeke. "Let's see how today goes, and we'll go from there."

"I can agree to that. At least you're not running."

"When did I run?" Had she done that to him?

"That wasn't the right word. Usually, you brush off my attempts to get to know you better."

"Sorry." She lowered her gaze. "I've recently come off a pretty bad break up." The jackass thought he could order her around in *and* out of the bedroom. He got a rude awakening.

"I'm sorry."

"Don't be. He was an ass." She glanced at the first bookshelf. Oh my. Alternative Lifestyles. Her heart pounded.

"Well, he didn't deserve you." He rubbed his thumb over the back of her hand. "Damon's bookstore is as tasteful as the adult store is."

"Oh, I've never been inside an adult store." In a way, that was funny. She'd dabbled in kink but never been into an adult store.

"I'd love to educate you, if you're willing."

"I might take you up on that, Mr. Riggs."

Chapter 2

Allyson Young stifled a yawn as she pulled her hair back. She'd stayed up far too late finishing up the book she was reading. It had been two weeks since the opening of the bookstore, and Allyson now went there at least twice a week.

Not only did Dani convince her to join the monthly book club, but dang if she hadn't gotten Allyson hooked on a romance author. Allyson was currently on book five of a long series. Not that she minded. The books had some kink in them, and she was loving it.

After securing her hair, she grabbed her storage clipboard and stepped out of her vehicle. She hadn't seen Zeke in those two weeks.

She stopped and gazed at the building. Eighteen months ago, this had been a dirt lot; now, a six-story building stood there. The new city executive building. Her lips tilted up.

"Right on time," commented a deep male voice.

Shivers ran over her skin as she looked up to see Zeke. His black hair curled at the ends, and his eyes regarded her with interest. Her nipples tightened. They hadn't gone beyond flirting when they met that

Sunday, but she was attracted to him.

"Zeke." Allyson fought to keep her tone even and professional. This was her job after all. Why did this man affect her this way? None of her old boyfriends made her skin tingle with awareness or caused her nipples to grow tight.

Work, Allyson. "Shall we do the final walk-through?" She pulled the checklist from her storage clipboard and fastened it to the top, trying to hide her body's reaction to him. Maybe she had been reading too many romances.

"Sure." He gestured for her to precede him.

See, all business. Good. Yet she noted how his long-sleeved work shirt clung to his broad shoulders and that it was tucked into his jeans. *Damn it, mind on business.* Zeke was being totally professional.

Allyson turned her focus away from Zeke and to her checklist as they walked through the building. She was acutely aware of Zeke beside her. Who was she kidding? She was always aware of him when he was around.

Flirting was one thing, but did he want more? Did she? She wasn't sure yet. But not knowing didn't stop her body from reacting to him.

As part of the City Planner's office, it was her primary job to make sure each stage of any construction was completed to specs. Pleasant Valley was still pretty small, under ten thousand people, so her job lines were blurred at times with other duties. At least that was one thing she never worried about with Zeke. He kept everything above code and was more than willing to show her invoices and work records.

So why had Rudy complained about the bookstore and all the trouble he had with Riggs Construction? Considering the other construction company headquartered in Pleasant Valley, Zeke was a dream to work with. Rudy was probably being an idiot.

"There's a plug cover missing," she said, pointing it out to him.

He blinked, and his gaze continued to focus in on her. Heat flowed from his gaze. "I'm sorry, what?"

So he was affected by her as well. Good to know. "Plug cover missing."

"I'll get that fixed right away." He gave her a smile.

Her heart kicked up at that sexy grin. He probably didn't mean it that way, but she forgot what to say next. She shook her head.

"It's minor." And it was, but she noted it. They continued their walk-through, and his gaze lingered on her each time she stopped to check things off. The awareness zinged between them.

Allyson breathed a sigh of relief as they reached the back door. Fresh air would be nice. She stepped out into the bright sunshine.

"Hey, Dani," Allyson said. Her best friend was kneeling on the ground tending to the plants.

"Hi, Allyson, Zeke." Dani stood up and dusted off her hand. "I'm finishing up with the plants."

"They look nice," Zeke said.

Allyson looked at the plants, bushes of some sort. They were small and looked good against the building.

"Drought resistant and they'll be easy to maintain," Dani said.

"Like we need to worry about a drought in the Pacific Northwest." Allyson laughed.

"You never know." Dani looked at Zeke. "Was there anything else you need me to do?"

"No, thanks, Dani. This was the last of it. Invoice me your costs."

His deep voice made Allyson's toes curl in her boots.

"Will do." Dani looked at her. "Meet for lunch at Sweet & Savory?"

"Sure." Today she could have a leisurely lunch with her friend, since her afternoon was filled with paperwork, which she could do in the office or at home.

"Great. I can't wait to discuss the book," Dani said.

Allyson's gaze went skyward. She so didn't want this discussion around Zeke. "Yep."

Dani smiled before gathering her equipment and making her way to her van.

She and Zeke followed at a slower pace. Allyson noted the even sidewalk and the striped parking lot. "Everything is perfect, as normal."

"It should be. So will your office be in this new building?" His eyes filled with curiosity.

Allyson laughed. "Nope. I'm stuck in the old

building, like the other peons. This is for the bigwigs."

"Oh." His eyebrows rose. "I would say you're as important as they are."

Allyson ducked her head. She wasn't good at accepting compliments. Her pen wobbled in her fingers as she signed the paperwork and tore off the pink copy at the back. "Here's a copy for your files."

"Thank you." His fingers touched hers, and sparks sped through her bloodstream. Allyson bit her lower lip, trying to convince her body this wasn't a good idea.

Maybe that wasn't quite right. Her body was ready. It was taking time for her emotions to catch up. Maybe they could have a fling? She tilted her head as she watched him. That would take some thinking about.

"I'll see you at the next job," she said as she turned and walked toward her vehicle. With each step, she could feel Zeke's gaze following her. When she got into her truck, she glanced at him to find he was still watching her with those perceptive eyes.

She waved at him as she pulled out of the parking spot. Once on the main street, she remembered to breathe. Zeke unnerved her at times, as he had for the last few years. He was far too attractive.

Allyson had learned years ago not to trust men. But there was something about Zeke that screamed, "trust me".

He got beneath her skin each time they met. No matter how she dressed, his gaze caressed her body. Even today, she had on a loose jacket over her work shirt, and she still felt the heat of his gaze. The day at the bookstore, he'd been the perfect gentleman. He'd shown her around and talked with her about books and reading choices. They never made it to the adult side of the store, but he'd seen to it she'd had a full education on what Damon's shop sold

She flipped on her truck's air-conditioning as her body flushed. Enough. She wasn't interested in a relationship with Zeke, and he didn't seem like the fling type. Better off to keep their relationship to business. Decision made, she drove to the next job site inspection she had with a twinge of regret.

* * * *

Zeke watched Allyson drive away in her small truck. She stirred his libido every time they met. He looked up to see his friend and co-worker, Gabriel, walk out of the building.

"All good?"

"Of course." Zeke grinned. He prided himself on making sure everything was up to code.

"What's next on the agenda?"

"I'm going back to base and meet up with the architect for Wicked Sanctuary." Max had been insistent that Gabriel draw up the plans.

Gabriel smiled. "That's going to be a fun project. I can't wait to work on it."

"Yep." Zeke couldn't wait to get started. When Max first asked him, Zeke had been humbled by Max's confidence in his ability. Yes, he'd done a lot of construction work since opening Riggs Construction four years ago, both residential and commercial, but the club was a special place.

"All right. After our meeting, I'm heading over to Damon's bookstore. Destiny called and said it looked like one of the shelves was pulling away from the wall, so I wanted to check it."

Zeke frowned. "That shouldn't be happening." He'd double-checked all the carpentry work himself.

"I know; that's why I'm going to look. Maybe it's a loose nail or something."

"All right. Meet up at lunchtime at Lara's café after you go to the bookstore? You can tell me what you found out."

"Will do."

Zeke jogged over to his truck. Now he would see the lovely Allyson again and see if he could make some headway with her. He thought after their time in the bookstore two weeks ago, she'd mellowed more toward him, but today, she was business as usual. He shook his head. Of course she was all business; they'd been on the job.

Maybe that was it. He needed to talk with her outside of business. He rubbed his chin. Maybe it was time to ask her out again before anyone else did. The thought sent a knot to his gut. No way was he going to allow another man to take Allyson out. He didn't go after her the last time, but he wouldn't make that mistake this time.

* * * *

Zeke strode into Sweet and Savory at twelve-thirty. His meeting with Gabriel about the club plans had been a good one. Gabriel added a few things, and the plans were almost done. Zeke would call Max this afternoon and set up a meeting to go over the final plans. Once Max approved them, he'd get with the planning office.

There was something else he would have to discuss with Max. While the club was known, he needed to talk with Max about the workers and others that would be around the club, which would include the staff from the planning office.

"Hi, Zeke," Lara said, walking up to him.

"Hey, Lara. You're busy today." The place was filled.

"Yeah. There's a table for four that's opened up; go take it."

"I can wait. It's Gabriel and me." Gabriel was finishing up at the bookstore.

"Go." She waved her hand in the direction of the table. "I know you and Gabriel will discuss business and need the room."

"Thanks." Zeke made his way to the table. He set his messenger bag and rolled-up plans on the empty chair and sat down on the chair next to it. He'd wait to order until Gabriel arrived and pulled out his phone to check his email. He lifted his head at the sound of feminine laughter — her laugh. Zeke turned.

Allyson stood by the door next to Dani with a wide smile on her face. Now why wouldn't she smile at him like that? She was relaxed, her shoulders straight but not tight, and that made his gut clench. With him, she was all business. He wanted more than business, but so far, Allyson had pushed him away, except at the bookstore.

Gabriel walked in behind the two women. Both turned their heads; Allyson smiled, but Dani's expression froze when she saw who it was. Interesting. As far as he knew, Gabriel and Dani hadn't met. Gabriel smiled at both women. Allyson pointed to a table that had just emptied and moved away from the pair.

Gabriel leaned down and said something to Dani. Her eyes widened, then her features turned hard. She said something and then walked away. His friend shook his head but watched Dani as she marched over to the table where Allyson sat.

"What was that about?" Zeke asked as Gabriel sat down.

Gabriel shook his head. "Nothing." But his gaze stayed on Dani.

Zeke decided not to probe, at least not right now. He'd get the story out of Gabriel later. "What happened at the bookstore?"

"Nothing big. It looks like a screw was missing. I fixed it right up."

"Great."

"So have you talked to Max about the plans?" Gabriel asked.

* * * *

"Why did you walk away and leave me with Gabriel?" Dani asked after she sat down.

"I saw an open table." Allyson noted her friend's flushed face. "What's going on?"

"Nothing." Dani glanced out the window.

"Gabriel and I dated in college."

"Oh?" Surprise colored Allyson's tone. "So he's the one you've been avoiding?"

"Yes." Dani waved her hand in the air. "Now tell me, what's new with you? We haven't had lunch in a week."

"Sorry about that." Usually, they had lunch together two or three times a week. "Last week was the week from hell."

"Rudy still causing issues?"

"Yep. He decided that I'm getting all the prime jobs. The main jobs I work on are with Riggs Construction. There are two construction companies headquartered in Pleasant Valley. They both pull in sub-contractors and others. I don't know what his problem is."

"He's a man."

Allyson laughed. "An ass is more like it." She glanced at the counter. It had thinned out a bit. "The usual?"

"Sure."

"Be right back." Allyson grabbed her wallet and got in line, trying to decide what she wanted today.

"Fancy meeting you here," Zeke said from behind her.

She flashed a startled look over her shoulder at him. "Not really. The café is very popular." He must have come in to have lunch with Gabriel.

"True." He looked over to where Dani sat. "Is Dani okay?"

"Why wouldn't she be?" Was he interested in

Dani now? Her stomach clenched. She refused to care. It wasn't like they had a relationship or anything.

"She didn't look happy when Gabriel spoke to her."

"I'm sure she's fine." It wasn't Allyson's place to discuss her friend's relationship with Gabriel, even if it was an old one.

"Good. Since we're both here, do you have some free time on your schedule this afternoon?"

"I might." Like bodies tangled in sheets time. Allyson closed her eyes at her lusty thoughts. That wouldn't do.

"Get that suspicious look off your face; it's about work." His brown eyes twitched with mischief. "Although I could take some time off if you had something else in mind."

His voice had dropped to a husky whisper that sent shivers of awareness over her skin. "What do you need…workwise?" She added the last word to make sure they kept things on a business level even if her libido yelled for a more personal afternoon.

"The new counters for the café expansion were finished earlier than expected. So if you have time to look at them and the new office area before you leave after lunch, it would speed up the rest of the process."

"I think I can spare some time." She hated paperwork; besides, it would keep her out of the office, and she wouldn't have to put up with Rudy.

"Good." The line moved. "Two-thirty good?"

"That's fine." It would give her plenty of time to have lunch and catch up with Dani. Allyson made it to the front of the line. She smiled at the young lady and ordered, then stepped aside.

She couldn't help glancing at Zeke as he ordered. He didn't flirt with the woman behind the counter, but he did smile at her. Well, of course he smiled; that's called being kind. Zeke stepped out of the way and behind her.

He was so close heat singed her back. Heck, she could smell his aftershave, all fresh air and pine. She turned slightly. His nose was straight; he had cheekbones a model would kill for, and his eyes twinkled when he looked at her.

"Here you go, Allyson." A tray was placed on the counter in front of her.

"Thanks." She reached for the tray.

"Let me." Zeke picked up the tray before she could close her fingers around it. He turned and carried it over to the table where Dani waited.

"You didn't have to do that," Allyson said when she caught up with him at the table.

"A gentleman always helps a lady." He winked at her after he set the tray down and left.

"Zeke is such a good man," Dani said as she unloaded the tray.

"I guess." Allyson took the empty tray and put it in the bin before taking her seat. But her gaze wandered to Zeke by the counter where he waited for his food.

"You guess? Allyson, do you need a doctor? That man is sex on a stick."

"What?" She stared at Dani.

"Come on, Allyson. You have eyes in your head. That man looks at you like you're his favorite ice cream cone, and he wants to lick you up."

She blinked at her friend. "But he's always professional on the job."

"Of course, you both are. But aren't you curious to date him?

"He asked me out before, and I said no."

"What?" Dani leaned forward. "When did that happen?"

"Once, while you were still in San Francisco, and again right after you came home. It's no big deal."

"Yes, it is. Allyson, we've known each other a long time. Don't let your past color what you could have with Zeke."

"I don't date anymore, remember? The complications aren't worth it."

"Zeke would be. Think about it."

Allyson nodded. Time to redirect this conversation. "I haven't seen you date since you came home." Her friend moved back to town when her grandfather became ill, to help her grandmother. Sometimes, Allyson envied her friend's grandparents. Being all but abandoned at as a child had left scars on Allyson's heart.

"I haven't dated because I haven't found anyone interesting yet."

She tilted her head and stared at Dani.

"All right." Dani ducked her head. "I haven't wanted to, but that doesn't excuse you. I've been back for close to a year. You, on the other hand…"

Allyson waved her hand. "I don't want a relationship. Dating means relationship. Now, let's move on to other subjects. Did you join Wicked Sanctuary?" She was aware her friend was interested in the lifestyle, as was she. But Allyson hadn't worked up the courage to take the first step.

"I did. Right after I came home."

"And I'm finding this out now?"

Dani giggled. "I wanted to test the waters so to speak."

"So how is it?" Allyson was curious. She'd been tempted to approach Max Preston and find out about joining, but fear of someone from her job finding out held her back. She could hear Rudy's snide comments now. A shiver crawled over her skin.

"It's great." Dani lowered her voice. "It's allowed me to let go of daily life and just be me."

"Sounds interesting." It did. Allyson couldn't remember a time when she wasn't in control. No, that wasn't right. When her parents abandoned her, she wasn't in control of her destiny, but after she turned eighteen, she never let anyone have control over her again. Which was why her last boyfriend was kicked to the curb when he tried to control her outside the bedroom.

Giving up complete control to a Dom outside the bedroom…she shivered. She wasn't sure she could trust anyone to that point.

"I think you'd like the club. I can check with Max and see if I can bring a guest."

"I'm not ready yet." She wasn't. She still had

some issues she had to work out in her head. "So what movie do you want to go see tomorrow?"

"Changing the subject." Dani grinned.

"Movie?" Allyson glanced over Dani's shoulder and saw Zeke's gaze on her. She lowered her gaze but not before the heat in his gaze scorched her body. Damn, why did her body seem to have a mind of its own when it came to him.

She concentrated on what Dani was saying and finished her lunch. It was bad enough she was meeting with Zeke afterward, but at least there would be others around to defuse the attraction. Oh yeah, she was attracted to Zeke and more. The question was: What was she going to do about it? One thing was certain: Resisting him was getting harder and harder.

* * * *

"So what do you think?" Zeke asked Allyson after they walked through what had been the old ice cream shop next to Lara's café.

"Looks good." She ran her fingers over the cream counters and checked the wood underneath.

"The office is over here." Zeke gestured to the framed doorway.

Allyson stepped inside and walked around. The electrical had already been inspected, so there wasn't much for her to do. She checked the framing of the room. It was sound. All of Zeke's work was. The man never cut corners.

"This is a nice expansion," Allyson remarked once they were back in the main area.

"It is," Lara said, walking up to them. "I'm super excited."

"Of course you are," a male voice commented. They all turned toward the door.

"Colby." Lara strode over to him and was drawn into his arms. Allyson looked away as they kissed.

"Embarrassed?" Zeke asked.

"They deserve some privacy." Allyson stared at the wall.

"What would you do if I kissed you like that?"

"What?" Allyson spun to face Zeke to find he'd moved closer to her, and she was practically in his arms.

"You and me kissing." His gaze captured hers. "Haven't you thought about us locking lips?"

Heat filled her cheeks, and she lowered her eyes. Yes, she'd thought about it and more. Zeke was front and center in her fantasies, but she wasn't going to tell him that.

Cool fingers touched her cheek, and she lifted her lashes to see Zeke staring at her. "I've thought about kissing you a lot." His voice dropped to a husky whisper. "While we're walking around on jobs, when you're eating lunch at the café and I see you, at night when I'm in my bed alone."

A gruff of laughter burst from her lips. "Alone? In bed? Do you truly expect me to buy that?" She'd seen the way women looked at Zeke.

"I do. You see…" Using one finger, he lightly stroked her hair. "All I can picture is your hair spread out on my pillow, your mouth open as you give little cries of passion as I make love to you."

Instead of shocking her, his words caused a tremor of anticipation to roll through her body. This wouldn't do. "Mr. Riggs,"—her voice was breathless—"you are being inappropriate." She stepped back even as her body protested the move. She was on the job and keeping those boundaries was important to her.

The teasing light disappeared from his eyes. "I am." He stepped away, putting more space between them. "My apologies, Ms. Young."

She hated when he used that polite, cool tone of his. "Look, Zeke—" she started.

"Hey Zeke, how much longer do you think it will take to get this place ready?" Colby asked, walking up to them with Lara at his side. "Sorry. Did I interrupt something?"

"No. Colby, this is Allyson Young with the building inspector with City Planning Office. Allyson, Colby Durham, owner of Durham's Leather shop."

Allyson held out her hand. "Very nice to meet you."

"Ms. Young." They shook hands.

"Allyson, please." Colby had a strong grip.

"We're probably looking at another two weeks. Since Allyson did a quick inspection for us today, things should proceed pretty quickly, provided we don't encounter any behind-the-wall surprises or supply chain issues."

"That's great," Lara said. "I was expecting a lot longer."

"You might need to close for a few days when we open up the wall."

"I was afraid of that." Lara groaned. "The café is so busy I hate to close for any reason. Plus, I need the Saturday for…ah…the catering job."

Lara had hesitated in her response, and Allyson wondered why. She glanced at the wall, then walked over to the plans Zeke had laid out. She'd been doing this job long enough that she'd picked up a few things. "You're only taking out a portion of the wall, right?"

"Yes." Zeke moved to her side. "What are you thinking?"

"Well…" She glanced up at him, and he nodded for her to continue. "Depending on where you plan to open it up"—she ran her fingers over the area on the plans—"if you take out this section, you could partition it off and pull it down overnight or on a Sunday when the café isn't open. Minimal interruption."

"Hmm." Zeke rubbed his chin as he studied the plans and then the wall. "That might be possible. I'll have one of the engineering guys look at it."

Zeke didn't shoot her idea down. Her admiration for him went up another notch.

"If that can happen, it would be great," Lara said. "Add any extra overtime to the bill. I expect Sundays and nights to be a higher rate."

"Yes." He glanced at the wall and then back to Allyson. "Thank you for seeing that."

"Anytime." Her cell rang. "Excuse me; I have to

take this." It was her boss. She stepped away from Zeke and across the room. "Hi, Wes."

"Are you coming back to the office this afternoon? I didn't see anything on your schedule."

"I can. I got pulled into an impromptu meeting at a client's site."

"Please, I need to talk with you."

Allyson's stomach clenched. "All right. Be there in about thirty minutes. Does that work?" She wondered what Rudy had done now. There was no other reason her boss would call her in.

"Take your time. And Allyson, you're not in trouble, so relax." The line went dead, and she shook her head. Was she so transparent?

"Everything okay?" Zeke asked.

She looked up to see Zeke, Lara, and Colby staring at her. Maybe she was transparent. "Fine. It was my boss. I need to head back to my office."

"Thanks for everything," Lara said.

"It's my job. But it looks really good, Lara," Allyson said.

"I'll walk you to your truck," Zeke said as he cupped her elbow.

"It's not necessary."

"It is to me." He guided her out of the shop and to the café parking lot where her truck sat.

"Is there another parking lot?" she asked. That could be an issue with the expansion of the café.

"Yes, on the other side of the ice cream shop and another lot behind the building." His smile made the day a bit brighter. "I made sure there was plenty of parking."

"Good man." She stopped beside her truck. "I guess I'll see you when I see you."

"Sooner rather than later, I hope."

Not sure what to make of his words, Allyson climbed into her truck and drove off. She waved at Colby and Lara as she drove past the café. Would she ever have a relationship as loving as theirs? She doubted it.

* * * *

"Is this a good time, Wes?" Allyson popped her head inside her boss' office within minutes of her returning to the main office.

"Come on in." He gestured to the chairs in front of his desk.

Allyson liked her boss. Wes had worked in the city planner's office for twenty years, and he knew most of the jobs inside out. She'd started in the permit office when she was twenty-three and worked her way up.

"How did the walk-though for the new admin building go this morning with Riggs Construction?"

"Perfect. Everything was in order and done to specifications, as always, so I don't see any reason why the move-in date has to change. But that's not why you called me in here." Allyson folded her hands in her lap.

"No. Look, I'm going to say it. Rudy is making noise about you always getting paired up with Riggs Construction."

Allyson shook her head. "Since Rudy and I are

your only certified inspectors for the city, of course we're going to work with the same company a lot. Rudy is usually tied up with Starr Builders when a Riggs Construction job request comes in. Besides, he recently did the bookstore, and the jobs are assigned to us. We don't get to pick and choose."

"I know." Wes sighed. "I've told Rudy it's a matter of who is available at the time. I wanted to give you a heads up: He's making a ruckus again."

"It's not like Rudy is quiet about his opinions." She'd heard him often enough in the break room, which was why she chose to take her lunch elsewhere.

"Right. If you have any issues with anyone, including Rudy, I want to know. I know you like to handle things yourself, but Allyson, I don't want Rudy to think he can start rumors without justification and get away with it."

"I will. Thanks, Wes." Allyson stood and walked out of his office and back to hers.

Rudy had come into the city planner's office two years after her. She'd been lucky to get one of the inspector jobs at twenty-six, compared to Rudy at thirty-eight. He hated that she had seniority on him in the office—and because she was a woman. Oh, yes, he'd said that to her face two years ago.

Technically, she could have taken it to Wes and HR and filed a complaint. She probably should have, but instead, she addressed it herself. Since then, Rudy had been out to get her.

In her office, Allyson sat down and logged into her computer. Since she was here, she might as well start on her paperwork. As she was inputting numbers, she realized that some of her last entries had been changed.

Odd. Maybe she'd put in the wrong information. She unlocked her file drawer and pulled out the file. Nope, the file had the right numbers. This didn't make sense. She matched up her handwritten information with that in the computer.

What the heck? She corrected all the incorrect information and saved it. Then she closed out the file and reopened it. The information didn't change. Okay, that was odd.

Shrugging, she submitted the new information on the county building and then input everything from today's meeting with Zeke at Lara's café expansion. When she finished, she checked her email.

Three new jobs, all from Zeke's company with a note stating Rudy had said he was too busy to take them on. She printed out the emails and made files for each. Monday, she'd call Zeke and set up appointments with him.

Allyson glanced at the clock, surprised to see it was almost four-thirty. She checked her schedule for Monday. She was meeting Zeke at one of his construction sites to go over a complaint the office received.

She frowned. Who was complaining about one of Zeke's jobs? She pulled up the complaint and all it said was, *not following environmental regulations.* That didn't make sense. She printed out the email and created a file, along with her checklist for complaints like this.

Monday was going to be busy. Not that she minded; she enjoyed her job. After locking her files up, she shut down her computer, picked up the bag that held her laptop, and went down the hall to her boss's office.

"Wes, I wanted to let you know before I leave I've received three more jobs for Riggs Construction."

"No worries. Have a great weekend."

"You too." Allyson gave him a wave and left the building. She sighed when she climbed into her truck. What was she going to do with herself tonight?

She'd swing by the grocery store first, pick up stuff for the weekend, and then spend a quiet night at home. She wondered what Zeke was up to tonight, then pushed the thought away.

Zeke wasn't on the agenda, even though her brain had other ideas. Nevertheless, he was never far from her thoughts that night, and that included her dreams.

Chapter 3

Zeke stepped out of his truck at Wicked Sanctuary at seven Friday night. Now that it was getting closer to summer, the days were staying light later. He took a deep breath, enjoying the smell of fresh pine.

Once he had his meeting with Max next week, he'd file for the permit to expand Wicked Sanctuary. He would need to discuss with Max how they wanted to handle the inspections. He trusted Allyson, but he wasn't sure about her co-worker, Rudy.

He'd caused so many issues with the bookstore, and he'd heard Rudy's snide remarks about the adult store. Not that Zeke was worried about people finding out about the expansion.

After Damon and Tessa outted the club at a press conference—with permission from Max—to stop Tessa's father from blackmailing her, Zeke was pretty sure there wasn't anyone in Pleasant Valley who didn't know about the club.

A grin formed. He enjoyed Wicked Sanctuary. It gave him a place to play and relax. Not that he'd played in a while. Some of the club subs still sought him out, but he found he wanted something more permanent.

Allyson's face popped into his mind. Yes, he wanted something with her. But he had to take baby steps. She was jumpier than a bunny. He pulled open the wooden door with the *WS* logo engraved on it to see Ralph behind the desk and…"Dani?" His breath caught in his throat.

When had Dani become a member? Why hadn't he noticed her in the club before? She was Allyson's best friend. Did Allyson know? Was Allyson interested in kink? Questions swirled around in his brain.

"Evening, Sir," Dani said.

"Evening, Zeke," Ralph said, glancing between the two.

"Ralph." Zeke kept his gaze on Dani while he signed in. "Would you mind if I steal Dani for a moment?"

"Of course not. But I do need her back. I'm showing her how the computer system works. She's my new assistant."

Zeke nodded and gestured to Dani to precede him down the hallway. "Classroom," Zeke said quietly as she walked in front of him.

"Yes, Sir." Her response was quiet and respectful.

Not that he expected anything less, but seeing Dani had thrown him for a loop. Once they were inside the classroom, Zeke looked at how she was dressed. She was wearing boy shorts, a sports bra, and heels. "When did you become a member, Dani?"

It was an obvious question. But he couldn't remember seeing her in the club during his on-duty times. Then again, there were a lot of people in the club when it was open.

"When I returned home, Sir."

"Drop the sir." Zeke shook his head, still grappling with the fact that Allyson's best friend was part of the club. A lot of people from town were members. "Why is this the first time I'm seeing you here?"

"I usually come in late on Friday or Saturday nights, mainly Fridays. Master Max was looking for someone to help Ralph, and I volunteered." She frowned. "Is there something wrong?"

Zeke stared at her. "Sorry, I don't know why I'm shocked at seeing you here."

"I'm sure you've seen other friends here," she said.

"Yes, but..." What? Just because she was Allyson's friend, and he lusted after Allyson. "You're right. Sorry, I reacted without thinking."

"It's okay." She smiled at him. "The club has gotten so busy, it's hard to know who's here and who's not."

"True. You'll be a great addition to help Ralph." He'd hired Dani for a couple of landscaping jobs. She was a hard worker, and he knew she'd do a good job.

"Thanks, Zeke. Now ask me the question you've been wanting to ask."

"What question is that?"

"Is Allyson interested in kink?"

Damn, how had she figured that out? Subs were tricky at times; they could read a Dom's face even better than a Dom could read them. "It doesn't matter." In that moment, he realized it didn't. He wanted Allyson regardless.

Dani smiled. "Allyson isn't as shy as you think. She's aware I'm a member, and I believe you escorted her around the bookstore on opening day."

"I did." Hell. He hadn't put it together until now. Allyson hadn't said anything as he escorted her around; she hadn't balked when he stopped in front of certain sections to talk with other people. She'd even picked up a book or two. "Well, damn."

Dani's soft laughter floated over to him. "Yep." With that, Dani scampered out of the room.

Zeke's breath caught in his throat. So Allyson was aware of the club and Dani being into kink. His mind spun in a thousand directions as he made his way into the men's room to dress for tonight.

Once dressed, he closed his eyes and centered himself. Tonight was a work night. But he couldn't get Allyson out of his mind. She always occupied some space in his brain. The way her hair framed her face, her bright eyes twinkling as they worked together. She'd captured his attention from the beginning. Now, he had to figure out how to get her to agree to a date.

He'd asked twice in the last couple of years, and she'd turned him down flat, but now… She'd been flirty at the bookstore and at the café. A grin overtook his lips. He'd see her on Monday, so he'd have another chance to ease his way into her good graces.

Once business was concluded, he'd ask her out,

even if just for coffee. He wanted to get to know her better, and baby steps meant a coffee date first. Mind set, he left the men's room and walked into the club.

Techno music was playing, and there was already a good crowd. Max stood by the bar. "Hey," Zeke said as he approached. Max was dressed in his typical black pants and a half-buttoned black shirt.

"Evening, Zeke."

"I know we're meeting next week about the plans, but I wanted to talk to you about how to handle the inspector and workers around the club."

"I've been thinking about that." Max set his water bottle on the cherry wood bar. "I can see how it might be an issue, but I think we can mitigate it. The club is open Thursday through Saturday, and they'll be here during the day, not after hours. We should be okay."

"True."

"Also, when they have to be inside the club, we can cover any equipment and make things look as vanilla as possible."

Zeke was impressed that Max had already thought this all through. "Workable. Once I get the plans approved by the city and have the permit, I'll set up an appointment with the inspector." Zeke rubbed the back of his neck.

"What's the issue there?"

"There's no telling which inspector we'll get."

"And one of them might be a problem?"

"Possibly. I worked with him on the expansion for the bookstore for Damon. He made some very snide comments."

"I see." Max stared over Zeke's shoulder. "Let's see who we get, but let me know about the first meeting, and I'll make sure I'm there. If he makes any snide comments, I'll let him know how unacceptable he is and call his boss."

"Perfect." Zeke rarely made complaints because he didn't want to stir the water. "Okay, I'm off to work." He walked away with a smile.

A few hours later, Zeke downed a bottle of water and watched the activities. He'd just come off shift as one of the monitors, and the club was packed tonight. It was a good thing Max was expanding. They were at capacity now.

He saw Dani talking with one of the Doms, and he took a step before he stopped himself. Dani was a big girl and didn't need him stepping in. Did he feel protective of Dani because she was Allyson's friend?

Allyson. His mind mulled over scenarios of getting her to go out for coffee with him. Monday couldn't come soon enough. A shout pulled him out of his head, and he didn't hesitate to head for the station the shout had come from. He might be off duty as a dungeon monitor, but he would make sure everything was okay.

* * * *

Monday came too soon for Allyson. She'd cleaned her apartment from top to bottom on Saturday, including getting her laundry done. All before she and Dani met up to go to the movies. Sunday was a reading day. Allyson had vegged out on her sofa with reruns on the TV and read the next book in the series

Dani got her hooked on.

Allyson was ready to start reading the next book, but unfortunately, she had to work. She sighed softly and opened her calendar program. She had a meeting with Zeke at one. Good. That would give her time to go down and pull everything for the new jobs she'd received on Friday.

Unlocking her file drawer, she pulled out the three files, relocked the drawer, and went down to the permit office. It took a few minutes to get copies of two of the permits; the other one hadn't been filed yet.

That was unusual. She normally didn't get a job until the permit had been filed, but it had happened before. Next, she went to the plans office to get them.

"Hey, Allyson," Debbie said when she walked in.

"Hi, Debbie, how are you doing?"

"I'm great. Thanks for asking. Who do you need plans for?"

"Riggs Construction, jobs 1646, 1792, and 1845."

"Be right back." Debbie disappeared into the next room. Allyson read over the permits and put them in their appropriate files while she waited. One for a residential remodel and another for a new building near the city limits. She didn't recognize the company name for the new building.

Debbie came back with her hands full and dumped the plans on the counter. "I've got two of them, the third one says the client is still confirming them. Job 1845."

"Okay." That was the same one that didn't have a permit yet. "Thanks." She gathered up the plans and went back to her office. She took the plans and put them in round cases for easier transport and then sat down at her desk and began inputting important dates on her calendar.

A knock on her door pulled her attention away from her work. A young man stood there holding a vase of flowers. "Ms. Young?"

"Yes." Allyson stood. Who could be sending her flowers?

"These are for you." He walked in and set the vase on her desk, then walked out before she could say a word.

Allyson studied the flower arrangement in the clear glass vase. There was a white envelope with her name on it. She plucked it from the holder and opened it.

"For a beautiful woman." She turned the card over. There was a Z on the back. A grin crossed her lips. Zeke? Who else could it be? It certainly wasn't Zorro. She giggled and reminded herself to talk with Zeke. This wasn't appropriate; it could look like a quid-pro-quo even though she suspected he did it because he wanted to and not for any other reason.

She studied the flowers. Purple sweet peas, red camellias, and several white roses. It seemed like an odd combination to her, but she knew someone who would know exactly what they meant. Allyson sat down and grabbed her cell phone.

"Hey Dani, do you have a few minutes? I have a question for you."

"Sure."

"I just got flowers."

"From who?"

"I'm pretty sure they're from Zeke, but I have a feeling they mean something. They're a combination I've never seen before."

"But you recognized the flowers."

"Oh yes. I do pay attention when you talk flowers."

Dani laughed. "Okay, what are they?"

Allyson told her about the flowers.

"Sweet peas mean blissful pleasure, red camellias for passion or deep desire, and white roses for new beginnings or the sender is worthy of you."

Allyson wrote down the meanings and stared at the paper. "Is Zeke trying to tell me something?"

Dani laughed. "Of course he is. Got to go, my client just showed up."

The line went dead. Allyson kept staring at the words. Could Zeke have known the meaning of the flowers? Or did he pick them out because he liked them?

Her office phone ringing caused her to jump. "This is Allyson."

"Allyson, Henry from closing permit office here. I was reviewing one of the jobs you submitted. Did you accidently hit disapprove instead of approve?"

She frowned. "Give me the job number." He did, and she pulled it up. "I don't know what happened. I know I approved it. Can you reject it, and I'll fix it?"

"Sure."

"Thanks for catching the issue."

"No problem. I know how closely you work with the general contractors and site supervisors, so your jobs almost always finish without problems. That's why this caught my attention."

Allyson hung up and waited until the job popped up as rejected. This was so odd. She pulled out her paper planner where she jotted down all the jobs she'd worked on in the last few weeks.

By noon she had checked every job she'd input in the last week. Several of them had changes she didn't make, others didn't. Something wasn't right. She had to meet with Zeke at one, so she'd talk to Wes when she got back.

Pulling out the file with the complaint in it, she locked up her laptop and put the file in her bag. Her stomach rumbled as she climbed into her truck. Thank goodness she kept a goody bag in her vehicle.

She grabbed a protein bar out of the bag and ate it as she drove. When she got to the site, she passed the gates, surprised to find protesters marching up and down the cleared lot. She found a parking spot a block away. Before she exited her truck, she looked at the complaint once again.

Environmental concerns. That was all it said. Maybe Zeke would know what was going on. Allyson put the file back in her bag and grabbed her hard hat. As she got closer, she was able to read the signs.

"Stop the thief of our green spaces," one read. Another said, "Natural resources can't be replaced." She bit her lip. Okay, environmental concerns. She knew this had to have been addressed when the plans first came through. Pleasant Valley was very strict about green space.

When there was a small break in the protesters' line, she slipped past them and onto the site. She saw Zeke talking with a group of men, but as she got closer, she realized they were arguing. Not good.

Zeke looked up and saw her. He motioned for her to wait, so she halted and waited for him. Within a few minutes, he walked over. He pulled his hard hat off and dragged his hand though his hair before putting the hard hat back on.

"Sorry about that," he said. "My guys aren't happy with the protesters." The crowd was now chanting after the silence when Allyson had walked through. "Let's go into the office."

Zeke took her by the arm and led her to the trailer that was their site office. Once inside, the sound of the chanting faded a bit.

"I don't know what to do about the protesters," he said as he took off his hard hat and hung it on the peg on the wall. "Have a seat."

"Why don't we go over what you're doing? I think there is some miscommunication going on." She took off her hard hat and set it in the empty chair. "You know about the complaint?" He should have received a copy.

"Yeah. I thought it was a mistake until I saw the appointment." He unrolled the plans over the large desk. "As you can see, I'm replacing all the trees, and there is going to be a big grassy area for the public." He pointed everything out on the plans.

Allyson looked them over. He was right. Something wasn't adding up. As she opened her mouth to ask a question, an awful noise filled the air, and the trailer shuddered.

"Stay here." Zeke didn't hesitate. He grabbed his hard hat and sprinted out of the trailer. Allyson ignored his order and grabbed her hard hat. She reached the landing of the trailer, and her heart lodged in her throat.

One of the large backhoes had turned over into a hole. Oh crap. Allyson pulled her phone out of her pocket and called for first responders. Zeke was gesturing for his men to move back as he stared at the backhoe. Then he moved closer.

Allyson gripped the railing on the trailer steps as Zeke climbed up onto the overturned equipment. What the hell was he doing? She wanted to yell at him to get down but was afraid of startling him and causing him to fall.

Sirens sounded. The backhoe shifted, and she barely stifled a cry of alarm. But Zeke adjusted his position and then reached inside the cab. He leaned back as he pulled the worker from the cab.

She held her breath until both men were safely on the ground. Zeke's men ran over to them, and guided them both away from the mess. The man Zeke had pulled out was limping, but otherwise looked unhurt.

"Really, boss, I'm all right." The man's voice carried in the quiet. She realized the sirens had been turned off, and the protesters were silent.

"I'm sure you are, but it's protocol." Zeke's voice

was loud and clear as the first responders rushed up to them. "Once they check you out and you're cleared, Lyle will take you home."

"Yes, boss." The man bowed his head as if he knew not to argue with Zeke.

Zeke glanced up and frowned when his gaze found her, but he nodded as if to tell her he was okay.

The men stepped back and allowed the EMTs to do their job. Zeke stayed close by until they were finished and left.

"Everyone go home; the site is now shut down," Zeke said.

The men groaned but started to make their way to their vehicles, Lyle helping the man who'd been in the backhoe to his vehicle. Zeke strode over the hard packed dirt to the trailer.

His gaze met hers, and without a word, he gestured for her to enter the trailer. She did. She put her hard hat back on the chair and turned to him. Zeke placed his hat on the wall, almost too calmly.

"You could have been killed." The words burst from her. Her heart was pounding. "That machine could have easily turned over, trapping both of you."

"Maybe." He kept his gaze on her. "It was fairly stable, and I had a man in there. I wasn't about to let him get hurt or trapped."

"What about you?" She marched over to him. "You could have gotten him out and then gotten trapped or killed yourself."

"You didn't stay inside like I told you to." His voice was gruff.

Allyson blinked. "What does that have to do with it? Damn it, Zeke! Don't you understand what could have happened?" Why was he grinning? The damn fool. Her temper rose.

"You care," he said softly.

"Of course, I care. I…" Her words trailed off. She turned away from him as the air was squeezed from her lungs. She cared, far more than she was willing to admit.

"Allyson." His voice was soft, and his arms encircled her from behind. "Thank you, but next time, I expect you to obey me."

"Obey? You didn't just say that to me." Memories of her ex-boyfriend surfaced. She pulled away from him.

"I didn't mean it that way." His voice held regret, and it froze her in place. "Please, sit down. I need to call the Industrial Accident Board, then we can talk."

He was right. They needed to talk, but he also had to report the accident. "Very well. But know this: I don't take well to being told to obey."

"So I noticed." There was a bit of humor in his voice.

She took a seat as he dialed on his cell. Allyson took several deep breaths, trying to concentrate on anything but the image of Zeke on top of that backhoe.

"Yes, he's been checked out and signed the release form." Zeke's tone was resigned. "I'll be here."

She'd been around enough accident boards to know they'd insist the worker see a doctor and ask for a drug test.

"They'll be here shortly," he said, his eyes dull. "Will you keep me company?" He rolled his shoulders and winced.

"You're hurt." Instantly Allyson was by his side. "Where does it hurt? Should I call a doctor?"

"I'm okay, just a twinge in my shoulder." He reached up and rubbed his right shoulder.

"Sit down."

"Now, who's giving the orders?" He took his seat, and she moved behind him.

"Sorry." She placed her hands on his right shoulder and began to massage. "You've got a good knot here."

Zeke groaned as she dug in. Allyson smiled when his muscles went lax. One thing she knew was massage therapy, since she'd taken several classes in college. Apparently, she'd retained quite a bit of it. "You should probably get checked out by a doctor."

"It's just a twinge. Probably strained something as I pulled my worker out of the cab."

"Possibly." She'd seen his muscles flex as he pulled the man out. She was proud of him for taking care of his men. He'd rushed right into the fray to rescue his worker without a thought for his own safety. While that scared her, she recognized the heroic actions as well.

His warm hand covered hers on his shoulder. "That was heavenly. Thank you." He captured her hand and pulled her around as he swiveled his chair.

"I can continue if you want."

"Not right now." He took her other hand. "I'm sorry if I scared you."

Her breath caught in her throat. He was apologizing to her? Men, in her experience, didn't apologize. "I'm sorry I yelled."

"I'm glad you did." He tugged her closer until she was bending over. "It showed me you care." He brushed a light kiss over her lips.

Allyson froze, but she didn't have to worry. Zeke backed off and let go of her hands. She instantly missed the feel of his skin against hers. She shook her head. They were supposed to keep their relationship professional.

"Go back to your seat, please." His voice was tense.

She tilted her head and stared at him.

"Don't make me beg, Allyson. I'm holding on by a thread here." He shifted in his chair, and her gaze caught how the fabric of his pants was strained around his crotch.

"Oh." Heat filled her body as she dug for something—anything—to distract them both. "Did the protesters leave?" She hadn't heard any chants since before the accident.

"Probably. They usually don't hang around once I send the crew home." He shifted in his chair. "So…this environmental complaint?"

"I have no clue why it was filed. Your plans show the green space. I didn't pull the plans from the office, but I will and double-check them. I wanted to check in with you first."

"Nothing has been changed, and these are the plans I filed."

"I know." She wanted him to know she believed him. Zeke was always above board with her. After seeing some of her entries changed in the system, she was beginning to wonder what the heck was going on. "Who was the initial contact on this project?"

"Rudy. Does that make a difference?"

"It shouldn't." A knock on the door startled them both.

Zeke stood. "That's probably the Accident Board."

"I should go." She reached for her bag.

"Stay." Zeke's voice was soft. "You were here when the accident happened."

"Let's see what they say first, and I'll stay if needed."

Zeke nodded and opened the door. "Mr. Riggs, Gavin Wilson, Industrial Accident Board."

"Please come in."

An older man walked into the trailer. Allyson had already made sure another chair was available for him. "Hi, Allyson."

"Hi, Gavin. Sometimes this world is small." Zeke stiffened, and Allyson glanced at him. His features were tight and a flare of jealousy flashed in his eyes.

"You know the IAB guys?" Zeke's gaze ricocheted from her to Gavin.

"Some of them yes. I met Gavin and his wife last year at one of the city parties, but I wouldn't say I know him." The jealous flicker in Zeke's eyes died out, and he grinned.

"We did have a good chat that night. Were you here when the accident happened?" Gavin asked.

"I was. Do you want me to stay?" Allyson shifted on her feet. Zeke was watching her with those deep brown eyes of his.

"No. I'd rather talk with Mr. Riggs first. I know where to find you, if I need to speak with you."

"Okay." She reached down and picked up her bag and hard hat.

"I'll be right back. I need to escort Ms. Young to her vehicle." Zeke pushed open the door for her. "The plans are on the table, and the accident site hasn't been touched."

"Thank you. See you later, Allyson," Gavin said.

"Bye, Gavin." She moved outside with Zeke right behind her. "You don't have to walk me to my truck."

"Yes, I do." At the bottom of the stairs, he cupped her elbow. "Will you have dinner with me tonight?"

"That probably isn't a good idea." Why was she saying that? Hadn't she thought about maybe giving him a chance?

"There's nothing wrong with a couple of friends going out to dinner."

"Is that what we are, friends?" She was thinking something more intimate. Allyson barely stopped herself from rolling her eyes at her wayward thoughts. A fling was good; a relationship was not.

"I hope we are." He reached up and ran his fingers over her cheek. "Please."

His please weakened her resolve. "Okay."

Friends. It was a dinner between two friends, nothing more. "Where and what time."

"The steakhouse at seven?"

"I'll meet you there."

His eyes twinkled as they made it to the gate.

"I'm fine from here on my own," Allyson said. She didn't need him to escort her. "Go get the interview with Gavin out of the way."

Zeke's lips turned up. "All right, but I'll stand here until you're in your truck."

"Fine." She turned and marched down to her truck. Zeke didn't move. She kept her movements efficient and precise to hide her annoyance at his hovering. Was she annoyed? Yes, but also thrilled he was attentive and caring. She started her truck and drove up to him.

"Satisfied?"

"For now." He grinned. "See you tonight." Zeke picked up her hand from where it rested on the door and raised it to his lips.

The contact of his soft mouth against her skin sent lightning bolts through her veins. Her breath caught in her throat. Zeke released her hand. One touch, that's all it took for her plans and her resolve to disappear into thin air.

She was in trouble.

Chapter 4

Zeke glanced at his watch for what seemed like the thousandth time in the last two minutes. *She'll be here.* It was five after seven. Allyson wouldn't stand him up, would she?

No, if she didn't want to have dinner with him, she'd have told him. She'd had no problems turning him down before. But what if she had an emergency? He didn't have her personal cell number, only her office number, and she had his main office number. He had a service answering the calls during the day, but not after hours.

He dialed his office voice mail. Nothing. Zeke drummed his fingers against the table. If she didn't show up soon, he'd go looking for her, but he didn't even know where she lived. He realized he was gritting his teeth in frustration. There was so much he didn't know about her.

"Can I get you something to drink while you wait, sir?" the waiter asked.

"No, I'm good." He actually wanted a whisky, but no hard alchol. Not tonight. The waiter left, and Zeke glanced toward the door. He stood as he saw Allyson striding toward the table.

"I'm sorry I'm late." She was slightly out of breath, as if she'd been running. "I can't believe the things that are happening in the office."

"You're here now." He held her chair out for her. Her eyes widened, then she sat, and Zeke resumed his seat. "Deep breath."

Allyson closed her eyes and did as he suggested. He watched the tension drain from her face after a few deep breaths.

"Better?" he asked as she opened her eyes.

"Yes, thank you." She flashed him a smile. "It was one of *those* afternoons after I got back to the office."

"I'm sorry to hear that." He glanced up as the waiter approached.

"Something to drink, ma'am?"

"Gin and tonic, please."

"Sir?"

"Beer, please. Whatever is on tap." The waiter walked away.

"I hope you don't mind that I ordered alcohol." Allyson's gaze was on him.

"I ordered a beer." He didn't peg her as a gin and tonic girl, but Allyson had some hidden depths to her.

"Not hard alcohol, like mine."

The waiter returned with their drinks. Zeke waited until Allyson took a sip of her drink before he spoke. "Want to tell me what happened at the office?" He knew sometimes it helped to talk about things.

She took another sip. "The plans you showed me at the site and the ones on file were different."

Zeke blinked. "That's not possible. I know I filed

the right plans."

"I'm sure you did." Her hand fluttered to the table as if she was stopping herself from reaching out to him. "I told my boss about it."

"What did he say?"

"He's looking into it. The green space specs were missing." Her fingers tapped against the tabletop. "The thing is, I can see faint lines that showed the green space."

"The complaint said environmental, but the protesters kept talking about taking away green space." He wondered who might want to do this to him. His former employer?

"Since the plans are publicly available by request, I'm assuming they saw them, hence the protest and complaint."

"Now what can we do?" He ran his hand around the back of his neck. He couldn't afford too many more delays. After the accident today, Gavin had given him preliminary clearance, but Zeke chose to close the site down while the board did their full investigation.

"If you get me copies of the right plans, I'll file them myself. Then we can post a notice at the construction site for the complaint, showing the new green space and the error on the plans has been fixed."

"Will that work?" He'd never had to deal with this before. Gavin had gone over the area and told Zeke it looked like a simple accident. He took some soil samples, but looking at the angle of the backhoe, he suspected some sort of mechanical issue had put the backhoe off balance.

Zeke was still concerned. He made sure all his equipment was inspected, but as Gavin reminded him, belts break without warning. Until the backhoe was lifted out of the hole, he couldn't tell for sure.

"It usually does." Allyson said.

"You've had these happen before?"

"Complaints and protesters, yes. Usually, I don't see the complaints, but this one came through to us because of the way it was phrased."

The waiter approached, and Allyson sighed. "I have no idea what I want to eat."

"Anything you don't like?" Zeke asked.

"Mushrooms, anchovies, that's pretty much it. Why?"

Zeke glanced at the waiter. "Give us a few minutes."

"Of course, sir." The waiter moved away.

"Will you allow me to order for you?" He was taking a risk here, but he wanted to see how she'd react.

"I'm not sure, Zeke." Confusion rushed over her face.

"I understand." While his Dom side was chafing at the bit, he pushed it away. As much as he wanted to take care of her, she was her own woman.

"Let's see." Allyson picked up the menu. "Is the prime rib good?"

She was asking his opinion. "The best."

"Okay, I'm ready."

Zeke signaled the waiter.

Allyson shut her menu. "I'll have the prime rib, medium well. Baked potato, butter only, and the seasoned vegetables."

"A salad to start?" the waiter asked.

"Caesar, please."

"Very good, sir?"

"Same, except my prime rib, medium, please."

"Of course, sir." The waiter took the menus. "I'll return shortly with your salads."

"Thank you," Zeke said, then he looked back at Allyson. "Was it my plans that caused you such turmoil this afternoon in the office?" He didn't like that he might be the cause of her being upset.

"It wasn't you. Lots of little things." Her fingers rubbed over the tablecloth. "Let's get off the subject of my job. Did everything go okay with Gavin?"

"He thinks it was an accident. That possibly a belt broke and sent the backhoe off balance and into the hole." He kept his gaze on her. There were lines of fatigue around her eyes he didn't like. "May I have your cell phone, please?"

"Why?"

"This way, next time you can call me and explain you're going to be late or that you're too tired for dinner."

"I'm not…" He stared at her. "Okay, I am a bit tired." She dug her cell out of her purse. "Wait a second. Next time? There isn't going to be a next time."

He wanted to protest, but he pushed it aside.

"What makes you say that?"

"Zeke, we're doing this as friends and just for tonight."

"Maybe." Not if he had his way.

Allyson closed her eyes and then opened them. There was regret shining in them. "If you want a fling, tell me, but I don't do relationships."

His eyebrows rose. "Oh?" He hadn't expected that from her. He was moving too fast, it seemed. "All right, let's keep it to friendship and friends having dinners together. And don't tell me you don't have friends."

"I do." She swiped her finger across her phone. "What is your number?"

He tilted his head and rattled off his number; the next thing he knew, his cell rang once and then stopped.

"Now you have my number."

Zeke laughed as he quickly saved her information to his phone. This woman was independent in more ways than one. "Thank you."

"You're welcome, but honestly, I agreed to this one dinner, nothing more. Zeke, we can't be seen like this."

"Like what? Two friends having dinner together?" What was she thinking? This woman was such a mystery at times.

She shook her head. "We both have professional relationships to maintain. Some might see this as inappropriate."

He frowned. "Do you?"

"It doesn't matter what I think."

"It does to me. Do you feel we can't separate business from personal?" He hoped that wasn't what she was saying. He didn't want to work with that Rudy guy, but if that was the only way he could see Allyson on a personal basis, then so be it.

"No." He blew out a breath, and she continued. "I'm saying others can't."

"Who cares about them?"

Allyson rubbed her forehead, and a part of Zeke wanted to drop this, but he couldn't. It was too important. If they didn't get past this hurdle, he'd have to make some major changes.

"I'm trying to understand." Zeke mentally moved heaven and earth to avoid revealing any of the frustration he was feeling right then.

"I know you are, and thank you. I'm being cautious."

"Is there a department policy that says we can't be seen outside of business hours?"

"Zeke, I'm sure you're aware of the conflict of interest here. I'm inspecting your building sites. This is going to get complicated."

"I understand, but we can figure it out. Let's get through dinner tonight and go from there."

She started to say something and then reconsidered and nodded.

Zeke relaxed in his chair. Crisis averted for now. Tonight would be a good starting place. "Why don't you tell me more about Allyson Young."

A bitter laugh escaped her lips. "Not the best

dinner topic."

Interesting response. He'd find out what she meant later. For right now, he'd let it slide. "How about if I talk about me?"

"Now that's a topic I can get behind." She grinned, and Zeke's dick jumped.

Down boy. She smiled. She didn't ask to touch you. "Let's see. I'm the oldest of three. I have a younger brother and sister."

"I'm an only child. So that's nice you have a brother and sister. Are your parents still living?"

"Yes." Allyson's must be dead for her to ask it that way, and the envy in her voice told him her childhood had been different from his. "Mom is a retired schoolteacher, and Dad is a retired electrician."

"You didn't follow in your father's footsteps?"

He chuckled. "Nope. From the time I was little, I liked to build things. I'd make things from blocks, later Legos, anything I could get my hands on."

"Sounds interesting. Tell me more."

* * * *

Allyson watched Zeke's face as he talked. So laid-back and happy. She was envious of his childhood. What memories she had of hers were anything but fun. She pushed them away. She was finally relaxing, and she didn't want old memories to intrude. Zeke did that for her. Helped her decompress and let go of the workday tensions.

In the back of her mind, the issues at work still nagged her, but not as bad as before. She'd left Wes a follow-up message because he'd left before she could talk to him. Tomorrow, she'd talk with him because things were not adding up.

As they ate, Zeke talked more about his teenage years and then college time. Then moved on to things such as books and movies. She was surprised to find they both loved action/adventure movies. Well, what man didn't? But he also liked those cheesy disaster films she loved to watch on late night TV.

"That was delicious," she said, pushing her plate away. "The prime rib was perfect."

"I'm glad you liked it."

"I did, and thank you for not lecturing me on how I like it cooked. I can't stand to have my meat mooing at me."

His husky laugh sent a shaft of awareness through her. It wasn't fair that his laugh could make her so aware of him and how sexy he was. Zeke hadn't put the kibosh on having a fling. She could be professional on the job and leave the personal out of it. She'd talk to Wes about it, because city regulations were a little vague. They talked more about accepting gifts.

"Dessert?" he asked.

"No, thank you. I'm full."

"Coffee or after dinner drink?"

"I'll never sleep if I have coffee, and the drink with dinner was enough. But don't let me stop you." He should enjoy whatever he wanted.

"I'm good." He raised his hand, and the waiter came over. "The check when you have a minute."

"Very well, sir."

"I never asked: how long have you worked for the city?"

"Almost eight years now."

"How does one get the job you have?"

"Hard work." She shrugged. She didn't mind talking about her job; it was her childhood she didn't want to discuss. "It sounds funny, but it's true. I took Urban Planning and Development classes in college. They took me only so far, so I started working in Building and Code Enforcement and worked my way through the system."

"Did you take other classes?"

"Mainly project management classes. I learned quite a bit on the job." She paused as the waiter dropped off the check, then pulled her wallet out of her purse.

"I'm paying," Zeke said.

"But this was a friendly dinner; I should pay my own way." Zeke stared at her. There was this thread of steel in his gaze that told her she was treading in deep water.

"My treat." His voice was low.

"Just this once." She didn't want to make a big deal of him paying. Heck, she and Dani took turns treating each other; this was no different. "You didn't mention where you went to college, just that you went."

"I ended up at MIT, getting my civil engineering degree in construction management." Zeke drew some money out of his wallet, put it in the portfolio, and stood. He held his hand out to her.

Manners. She'd forgotten what it was like to be around a man with manners. Most of the guys she worked with treated her like another guy, except Rudy. He was an ass. But Zeke reminded her of what a real man with manners was like. He guided her out of the restaurant.

"Where are you parked?" he asked.

"Third row, toward the end." He nodded, and they walked to her truck. Allyson turned when they reached her vehicle. "I had a great time. Thank you for dinner."

"I had a great time too." He gazed down at her. "My truck is in the next row. Wait until I come up behind you before you back out and leave."

She opened her mouth, but he placed his finger over her lips. "I'm going to follow you home to make sure you get there safely."

Her lips tingled from his touch. "There's no need."

"There is to me." His gaze held hers. "I'd do it for any woman who drove herself."

Allyson stared at him. There was something in those chocolate brown eyes of his. Concern? Maybe. Determination? Probably. "All right." She'd allow him to follow her home. It was better than arguing in the parking lot. Allyson ignored the shaft of warmth flowing through her body at his concern.

"Thank you." He waited until she climbed into her truck and shut the door before he made his way to his vehicle.

Allyson's insides swelled with something new.

Gratitude? Hope? Need? All were possible, but this was more. Zeke pulled up, and Allyson backed up. Then, with him behind her, she drove out of the lot.

His small gesture of making sure she got home safely made her feel special. *Stop it.* He said he would do it for any woman. She parked in her assigned spot at her apartment building and saw Zeke pull into a visitor spot.

"I'm home," she said as he climbed out his truck.

"I know you are." He cupped her elbow. "But I always escort my date to her door."

"But this wasn't a date, just friends having dinner." Her insides tightened.

"I'd do the same for my friends."

Allyson stopped herself from rolling her eyes as she swiped her card through the card reader to open the door to her apartment building. It was one of the reasons she'd chosen to live here: more secure. Not that Pleasant Valley was a hotbed of crime, it wasn't. She needed the security.

"I'll walk you to your apartment door," Zeke said, following her inside.

She didn't argue with him because she was pretty sure he wouldn't leave until he was satisfied. A tiny giggle escaped her lips before she could stop it. Zeke was forceful; dare she think…dominant?

Her nerves tingled. She stopped in front of her apartment. Another reason she liked this apartment building, single level. "This is me."

"I'd normally not ask, but will you allow me to open the door and make sure everything is okay?" He held his hand out for her keys.

Allyson tilted her head. "Why wouldn't it be?"

"Please."

He was being very protective. This man would never let his woman be afraid or fear she could be attacked. Allyson shook her head. Where had that thought come from?

"Okay." She dropped her keys into his palm with the knowledge she was allowing him to do things she'd never let another man do for her. "Third key for the dead bolt, the second key for the door itself."

"Thank you." Some of the visible tension left his body.

Allyson's tummy did a funny summersault as he opened the door. She'd never had a man in her apartment before. "Light switch on the right." The lights flared.

"Stay here, please." There was that *please* again. Her insides melted. Zeke slipped inside and, within a few moments, was back. That didn't surprise her. Her apartment wasn't that big. "All clear." He held her keys out to her.

"Thank you." She was still a little perplexed why he felt the need to check out her apartment, but her nerves were doing a little dance at his attention.

Zeke grasped her by the shoulders and turned her so her back was to her apartment. "I had a wonderful time tonight."

"I did too." Hadn't they said this earlier? Her heart was doing a strange tattoo in her chest.

"I'm going to kiss you, Allyson. If you don't want

me to, tell me."

She swallowed. Words dried up in her throat, and she went up on her toes.

Warm lips closed over hers. The kiss was soft, not tentative but not aggressive either. It was over before she could analyze more.

"Good night. Go inside and lock the door."

"Bossy." Her voice was soft and breathless. He did that to her with a kiss. Wow.

"Always around your safety."

Allyson didn't argue and slipped inside her apartment, shut and locked the door. She kept her hand against the wooden door for longer than was necessary, as if she could still feel Zeke's presence.

What was wrong with her? Zeke was a good guy, but she didn't want or need a man like him in her life. She should have objected to the kiss, but she hadn't. She turned and caught the scent of the flowers she'd brought home from work.

She forgot to ask him about that. The flowers were beautiful. Well, the next time she saw him outside of work, she'd thank him for them. Wait…what was she thinking? She wasn't going to see him outside of work again. *Coward*, a voice inside her muttered.

"Self-preservation," she said out loud. No one she loved stay around her for long. They all left. Well, except for Dani. She came back. But Zeke wouldn't hang around. Men didn't. And there was no sense in starting something that would end with someone being hurt. That someone being her.

* * * *

Zeke grinned the entire drive home. Allyson didn't get upset with his need to make sure she was safe. She was so independent he wasn't sure how she'd handle it, but she did great. Dinner was a success, except for the part where she kept insisting they were just friends.

He wanted to smash in the face of whomever hurt her and made her think she couldn't have a relationship. His fingers tightened around the steering wheel. He'd get to the bottom of that and why she didn't want to talk about her childhood.

Tonight was the first step in his campaign. He was going to win Allyson over to his side. Zeke paused in his thinking. He didn't know enough about her yet to be thinking long-term relationship. A step at a time. He understood her worry about them working together, and he'd show her he could separate work and pleasure.

His smile grew wider. Wait until she saw Wicked Sanctuary. That would be a good way to judge how she felt about a kinky lifestyle. Not that it was that big a deal for him. He was comfortable keeping their kink to the bedroom. And he was getting ahead of himself again.

First, get her to agree to a relationship and then on to kink.

Chapter 5

"Are you sure?" Wes asked Allyson the next morning.

"Yes." Allyson shifted in her seat in front of Wes' desk. She'd pulled up several jobs this morning before this meeting and found stuff had been changed. "I even took screen shots." She handed them to Wes. Thank goodness she had the foresight to do that.

"Well, I'll be damned. Let me get IT on this. They should be able to trace it."

"All right. I've changed all my passwords to be on the safe side. But this is very concerning, Wes. Someone was also able to change the plans on one of the Riggs jobs."

"How do you know that?"

"I received a complaint about environmental concerns."

"All of those are supposed to come through me."

"I know. I assumed I got it because you sent it to me and because I approved the original plan. It was an empty lot when the plans came in. I reviewed and approved them. So when I got the complaint, I followed up with Riggs Construction and met with them yesterday afternoon."

"What did you find?"

"Besides protesters? I talked with Mr. Riggs, because I'm aware he's environmentally conscious. All his jobs include green space, so it didn't make sense. It wasn't until I saw his plans that the complaint didn't make sense."

"Maybe Riggs filed the wrong ones."

Allyson shook her head. "I would have thought that too if I hadn't seen the originals. I pulled the plans when I got back yesterday. All the green space was missing. Something is off, Wes."

"I agree. Anything else?"

"No. But did you see I received a Starr Construction job?"

Wes nodded. "Rudy claims he's overloaded."

Allyson prevented herself from snorting at the comment. More like he didn't want to do the work. "Right." With that, she left Wes's office and went back to her own. She stopped short in her doorway.

There was a teddy bear with balloons sitting on her desk. She glanced over her shoulder. Someone must have delivered it while she was in Wes's office. Allyson snatched the white envelope sitting in the teddy bear's arm with her name on it.

She ripped it open. *To a beautiful lady, may this make you smile, and remember I'm nothing but a big teddy bear. ZR.* Laughter burst from Allyson's lips. Zeke thought he was a big teddy bear? She loved the gesture, but he couldn't do this. Someone was going to get suspicious or call it out.

"Well, well, well, it looks like someone has an

admirer," Rudy said, lounging against the door frame to her office.

Her good mood vanished. "What do you want?" She tucked the card away in her pocket and moved the bear and balloons off her desk onto the small side table. At least he thought she had an admirer.

"I understand you got a Starr Construction job."

"Yes, but I haven't looked at it yet."

"Be sure you give them plenty of notice when you want to meet up. They're not as *accommodating* as Riggs Construction is." Rudy's smarmy comment wasn't lost on Allyson.

She ground her teeth together so she wouldn't make a smart-ass remark. "I'll keep that in mind. Now if you'll excuse me, I have work to do."

"Sure." Rudy left, and Allyson wondered why he'd even stopped by. Probably to get under her skin. She rolled her shoulders, and the teddy bear caught her attention. A smile crossed her lips, but she'd have to talk with Zeke about sending her presents to the office. It wasn't professional.

* * * *

A week later, Zeke glanced around the café expansion. It was almost done. After talking to the engineer about the wall, they'd had to change the position of the door between the two cafés, which had changed the plans somewhat from what the originals. Not unusual. There were also a few other changes.

He'd already talked with Allyson and asked her if she could meet him at the job so they could discuss the changes. He had the new plans in hand and would file them once he talked with her. He was going to make sure all his jobs were on the up and up. Not that he hadn't before. But if he was going to convince Allyson to take a chance on him and keep seeing him outside of work, then he had to make sure to keep their work time to work.

At a knock on the door, he raised his head from where he was studying the plans. There she was. His heart skipped a beat. He took in her jeans and work boots, then moved to the dark blue long-sleeved shirt, and the smile on her lips. He grinned as he strode to the door and opened it.

"Right on time, as always."

"I try to be." She slipped on a white hardhat as she stepped through the door and glanced around.

Zeke couldn't stop smiling; he was so happy to see her. He had to fight the urge to enfold her into a big hug.

"This turned out nice." She looked around before pushing a strand of hair behind her ear as she gazed at him.

"The vinyl flooring was one of the last pieces, but we did have a few changes." She looked adorable in her white hardhat, and while her long brown hair was pulled back, strands kept escaping. "Let me show you." He gestured to the makeshift table where the plans were laid out. "I thought it would be easier to go over them before I filed them."

"Sure." She adjusted her hardhat, and he grinned.

"I talked with the engineer about the wall and your suggestion. We had to move the doorway between the two, which meant changing a few other things. We moved the office." He pointed to the spot on the plans and then to the newly redone office. "The freezers will be moved down, and there will be more counter space."

She glanced up and took in the location of the new office and how the freezers were arranged. "I'm assuming the electrician double-checked the voltage and made sure everything was good?"

"Yep. Have his report here." He slid the papers out from underneath the plans and handed them to her. He kept his gaze on her as she read the report. "It was a good thing this was an ice cream shop before. Most of the electrical was already set up for freezers." She looked at the plans. "It looks like you lost some table space."

"A little bit. I talked with Lara. We're losing roughly four tables, but she's okay with it as it will give them more room behind the counters and the freezer space is bigger.

"And the doorway?"

"Yes. Going with your suggestion, we moved the doorway so when we pull down the wall between the two places there won't be any problems."

"Since the electrical inspection has been done, and everything lines up, go ahead and file the plans. I'll make notes in your file, but it all looks good."

"Will do."

She straightened up from the plans and looked at him. "I need to change the subject for a moment and move to a more personal topic."

Zeke froze. Her tone was serious and her expression filled with worry. "Sure. What's up?"

Allyson glanced down at the floor, before meeting his gaze once again. "I need you to stop sending me gifts at work."

Her cheeks turned pink, and Zeke had to bite back a grin at how adorable she looked. "Are the gifts not to your liking?" While she'd texted him her thanks for the bear, they hadn't really talked, mainly because he'd been busy between his company and then working at Wicked Sanctuary.

"It's not that." Her teeth worried her lower lip. "Zeke, it could look like a bribe to some people in my office. We're not allowed certain gifts. I have to make sure no one thinks we're not keeping things on the up and up."

He remembered the talk. No big-ticket items, but these were small things, nothing that broke the rules. "Who is having issues?" He stiffened.

"It doesn't matter." She shook her head.

"It does to me." He didn't like the idea of someone thinking of her being unprofessional. "Those gifts are between two friends."

"Is that what we are? Friends?"

"I'd like it to be more." A lot more. But he didn't want to scare her away. If friendship was all she would accept, he would take it.

"I'm not sure I can do that." She sighed. "But no more gifts. It could look like a quid pro quo."

He swore silently. "Is your boss making accusations?" He didn't like the idea of someone making Allyson feel she was doing something wrong. She wasn't. They weren't.

"Not my boss." She scuffed the toe of her boot and looked at the floor.

"Allyson." He kept his tone soft and soothing, even if his dominant side was chaffing at the bit to get the entire story. "We're doing nothing wrong. I want to get you to know you better."

"I'm still not sure that's a good idea."

"Why not?" He was perplexed. They'd had a good dinner a little over a week ago; she admitted she liked his gifts, and the kiss they shared had been the tip of the iceberg. He hadn't pushed this last week, maybe that had been a mistake.

She lifted her head and stared at him. Ah, there was that flare of independence.

"I explained why it's not a good idea. We have to keep things above board. The mere appearance of something improper can set someone off."

"You also said it wasn't your boss who was making you uncomfortable. I'll stop sending you gifts to the office. What else is bothering you?" He wanted to get to the bottom of this.

"I'm not good dating material," she muttered.

"What?" He stared at her. "Not good dating material?" He shook his head. Who'd made her feel this way? "You said we're friends, right?"

"Yes."

"Then let's be friends outside of work. Friends go to dinner and get to know each other."

"But—"

He placed his finger over her soft lips. "I will be nothing but professional on the job, just like you are, but off the job, I want to get to know you. And if things progress from friendship to more, then we'll deal with it."

Her cheeks bloomed red, and she shifted from one foot to the other. There was indecision in her eyes. He dropped his hand.

"Allyson, I've been attracted to you for a long time now."

"I know."

"Until last week, you've always turned me down when I've asked you out."

"True."

"After the bookstore opening, I thought you were ready for us to at least be friends."

"I am." She lifted her chin. "When you asked me out last year, I was still involved with someone. That's why I turned you down."

"Are you saying you're still involved with him? Or maybe it was her? I shouldn't assume."

Her laughter was music to his ears. "It's a him, and he's out of the picture."

"I'm not seeing anyone either." Before he asked Allyson out that second time, he'd broken off his relationship with Melanie, one of the club subs. She'd started to want more than he wanted to give her.

"I'm still not sure."

"I am." He didn't want to crowd her, so he stepped back. His Dom side yelled at his withdrawal, but something told Zeke it was the right thing to do.

"How about dinner Wednesday night?"

Her eyes brightened, and Zeke was elated he was on the right track with her. She wanted to go out with him. Friendship first, then he'd move on to a relationship.

"All right," she whispered. "But not too late. I have an early meeting Thursday."

"Done." She looked at him. Her eyes softened. "Before we go back to work, I'm going to kiss you." He placed his hands on her shoulders.

"Do friends kiss?" There was a saucy tone in her voice.

"I kiss my friends all the time."

She nodded and went up on her toes, raising her lips to his.

Zeke groaned as his mouth closed over hers. Those soft lips tasted of cherries.

He slipped one hand to her neck to cradle her head as he teased her lips with his tongue and mouth. She was pliant in his hold until her hands fluttered to his chest. She didn't push him away; instead, her palms ran over his shirt to his shoulders.

Don't scare her, he warned himself. He drew his tongue over her lips before lifting his head. Her eyes were closed, her breathing not quite steady. Her lashes fluttered, and her eyes had a dream quality to them.

He fought back the overpowering need to pull her into his arms and kiss her until neither one of them could breathe. Zeke closed his eyes and took a deep breath.

"As much as I hate to stop, we both have jobs to get back to." Everything in him protested his words, but it was the right thing to do.

She blinked several times before she came out of her dreamy state. Color flared high in her face and neck. Allyson took a step back, and her arms fell from around him. He missed her touch, even as light as it was.

"None of my friends kiss like that."

Zeke chuckled. "Wednesday, I'll pick you up at six."

"I can drive myself."

He titled his head and stared at her, not saying another word.

She sighed. "That's fine."

"Thank you."

"Make sure you file those new plans. And have a good rest of your day." Allyson turned on her heels to walk to the door.

"Bossy much?" Zeke said.

She stopped and turned back to him. "When it comes to getting these jobs right, you bet." She continued on her way.

"Allyson," he said when she pulled the door open. "See you Wednesday."

"Bossy much?" she quipped, turning his words back on him.

He grinned. "You have no idea."

Allyson rolled her eyes before walking out and closing the door softly behind her. She had no idea how bossy he could be. But she'd find out once they got past the friendship part of this relationship and only if she was willing.

* * * *

Allyson looked at her closet and then back to her bed. She had clothing everywhere. She sighed. This was not good. It shouldn't be this hard to find something to wear to dinner.

Zeke had texted her that he was going to take her to the Double D BBQ, so dressing should be easy, but it wasn't.

"Come on, Allyson," she said out loud. "You're not trying to impress him or anything. This is friends going to dinner." With a shake of her head, she grabbed a pair of black jeans and one of her embroidered tops.

She put the rest of the clothes back in her closet and glanced at the clock. Five-thirty. Damn. A quick brush of her teeth, a splash of makeup, and she was back in her bedroom to dress.

She'd just slipped on her sneakers when the doorbell rang. Allyson ran to the box on the wall by the door. "Yes."

"Good evening, Allyson," Zeke's voice sent shivers over her skin.

"Opening the door." She pressed the button to buzz him in. Allyson closed her eyes, took a deep breath, and blew it out before she opened her apartment door. "Hi," she said when he approached.

"Hi." He leaned down and brushed a soft kiss over her lips. "You look delicious enough to eat."

Allyson gripped the metal door handle to stop

herself from launching herself into his arms and deepening the kiss. *Oh girl, you got it bad. Remember you're the one who insisted on friendship, not a relationship.* She stepped back. "Come on in while I get my purse."

"Thank you." His voice was soft as she turned to get her purse from her bedroom. It wasn't like he hadn't been in her apartment before. But she still hurried to grab her purse off her dresser.

Zeke was still standing by the door, but his gaze moved around her apartment. "It's small but I like it." Why did she feel embarrassed by her apartment size? Maybe because Zeke was a big man. No, that wasn't quite right. He was very fit, well built and…all those muscles.

"It suits you." He opened the door.

"Thank you." She locked up after they stepped out, and he guided her to where his black truck sat in a visitor parking spot. Like a true gentleman, he opened the passenger door for her. Allyson pulled herself up into the cab and then reached for her seatbelt.

"Everything at work going okay?" he asked as he pulled away from her apartment complex.

"Yes." Rudy had been out of the office the last few days, so she hadn't had to deal with him, and there hadn't been any more changes to her files, so maybe IT had figured out the problem. She'd also told her boss they needed to discuss the city policy on fraternization, but Wes had been tied up in meetings.

Silence fell. She didn't know what to talk about.

Maybe this wasn't such a good idea after all. What did they have in common besides work and some books and movies? Dread settled in her stomach.

Once at the restaurant, Zeke parked the truck and helped her from it. Together, they walked into the restaurant.

"Hey, Zeke." Tina gave him a smile.

"Hi, Tina. I made a reservation."

The bubbly blonde looked down at the podium. "I have it right here. If you'll follow me." She grabbed some menus.

Zeke gestured for Allyson to precede him, and she followed Tina to a table by the window. Except it wasn't set up with the chairs across from one another, but side by side.

"Thanks, Tina." Zeke held out the chair closest to the window for Allyson.

Allyson sat down, and Zeke took the seat next to her.

"Mike will be here to take your drink order shortly. Enjoy." She set the menus down and walked away.

"Do you come here a lot?" Allyson asked, picking up the menu. She'd counted on Zeke being across from her. With him next to her, she could feel his warmth, and it made her want to curl against his body and hug him tight.

"Usually at least once a week. Most of the time, I grab and go."

That explained how the hostess knew him by name. "They must have good food." Right now, food was the last thing on her mind. *Come on, Allyson, get your act together. Friends, remember?*

"You've never been here?"

"For some reason, I haven't."

"Then if you'll allow me." He plucked the menu from her fingers. "I know just what to order."

Allyson was about to protest but held it back. Why not? "All right, but nothing spicy, especially the barbecue sauce."

"Got it." He grinned as the waiter arrived.

"Good evening, I'm Mike, your waiter for tonight. Would you like something to drink?"

Zeke looked at her.

"Do you have a pale ale on tap?" she asked.

"I do."

"That will work."

The waiter looked at Zeke. "I'll have the same."

"Very good. Are you ready to order?"

"Yes."

Allyson glanced out the window, only half listening, while Zeke ordered. Robins mingled in the trees outside the windows. They chased each other, and she couldn't stop smiling at their antics.

"Bird watching?"

Zeke's voice in her ear made her shiver. "They're pretty, but did you know they don't mate for life?"

"True, they don't. But they do spend an entire breeding season together and usually come back together every season."

She turned her head to find Zeke so close her cheek brushed his. Heat flooded her body. The retort she had on her lips died, and her mind went blank.

"Tell me, Allyson, are you interested in being more than friends with me?"

Yes, her body yelled. "I need some space, please." She placed her hand against his chest trying to ignore how soft his shirt felt beneath her fingers, and how hard his chest was, and how she wanted to slide her hand up into his hair and tug him down for a kiss.

Zeke leaned back, and she took a breath. Now his question. Was she interested in more than friendship? She was, but fear of him leaving her surfaced. What to tell Zeke? The truth. She promised herself a long time ago to always tell the truth.

"Yes and no." Fire flared in his eyes, making them glow.

"Explain."

"The no revolves around people seeing us working together and having a relationship as a conflict of interest. You do realize that my boss could remove me from all your jobs?"

"We'll deal with that if it happens. But I won't cross that line between professional and personal from now on." He lifted his hand and touched her cheek. "I mean it, Allyson. Work is work. When we're on the clock, it's professional. Off the clock? Well, that's between us and no one else."

"Can you keep them separate?" She could, but then there would always be people like Rudy who thought it inappropriate. Why did it matter so much to her? Rudy was an ass, and she had a right to a life outside of work. Heck, she knew of at least three couples. Two were married. One worked for the city, and the other contracted with the city. And one of the women in permits was dating an architect two cities over. First thing tomorrow, she'd let Wes know she was seeing Zeke outside of work hours.

"I can. At work, you're Allyson Young from the inspection office, but at night, when we're together, you are Allyson, my lady."

"Your lady, huh?" Why did his words make her feel special? Cherished? How was it Zeke got beneath her exterior and turned her to mush?

"If you want to be."

Allyson bit her lip to stop herself from saying, *I'm already yours.* The words wanted to burst from her lips, but now was not the time. "Let's take this one step at a time. You're being… What's the word I'm looking for?"

"Dominant."

"Yes. Dominant. You're very dominant at times." She hadn't thought about it like that. A tremor of excitement went up her spine. Was he into the lifestyle? Oh, this could get complicated — in a good kind of way.

"I am." He stroked her cheek, and she enjoyed the feel of his rough fingers against her skin. She wanted to melt against him.

Get a grip. Let tonight play out and see how things work out and go from there. They had time.

Their waiter set their beers on the table and walked away. Zeke shifted in his seat, giving her some much needed breathing space.

"Does your dominance go beyond ordering dinner and making sure my apartment is safe?" What prompted her to ask that? Because she couldn't stop her runaway mouth, that's what. And don't forget about reading all those romance books. Yes, she admitted to reading them and fantasizing about a man coming into her life. Darn romance heroes. All the men she'd dated had failed painfully to measure up to her standards and ended up being not much more than jerks.

But those book heroes were the fantasy. In real life, if a man tried to order her around, she'd hit him over the head with a frying pan before she kicked him to the curb. Her lips curved up. She'd put a few Doms in their place when she used to attend play parties, especially when they assumed too much.

Zeke shifted closer, and Allyson gazed into his eyes, seeing fire there. She blinked. That wasn't really possible, but damned if she didn't think for a moment she saw flames.

"I'm going to be honest here. I'm dominant in the bedroom, if that's what you're asking. In other aspects, I'm protective of those I care about."

His words sent a tremor of excitement and apprehension through her. Not because of the bedroom, but his protectiveness. She swallowed hard.

"I've scared you," he said as he lifted his hand to cover hers where it lay on her thigh.

"Not really." Okay, maybe she wasn't telling him everything, but he didn't scare her.

"This is a talk we need to have. We're in a public

place where I want you to feel at ease, but I also wanted us to have some privacy, which is why I requested the table be set up like this."

Allyson glanced around. There were other couples sitting together like them, but unlike their table, the others four chairs, while theirs only had two. It was then she realized there was no one seated next or behind them.

"How did you get them to leave the tables closest to us empty?" He'd gone to a lot of trouble to make her comfortable.

"I'm not going to answer that right now. Just know I'd move heaven and earth to make you feel comfortable with me."

Her breath shuddered in and out. "What kind of talk did you need us to have?"

"Whether we can move past friendship and on to a relationship."

Her first impulse was to push away from him, but she was going to be honest with him and herself. It was time. Her heart did a rapid tattoo in her chest.

"We can move to a relationship." Relief spread over his face, and his shoulders visibly relaxed. He'd been tense; she hadn't realized.

"This next question is a little more intimate." He leaned down. "How do you feel about kink?"

Heat swept through her. *Oh my God, Zeke was kinky?* "It depends on your definition of kink. I'm not into the slave/master type of stuff."

"That I could have guessed. I'm not either. More into the Dominance/submission. The deep relationship between Dom and sub that can form a bond of trust like nothing else."

Allyson sucked in a breath. Was he talking about a power exchange? She thought that was a myth. She'd never seen one in her years at the play parties. Would she recognize one if she saw it? It was one of the reasons she stopped going. She wanted something deeper, more meaningful.

"All right." This was new territory for her. She'd talked with a Dom at a play party and negotiated before they played together, but that was usually a one-night type of thing. Zeke wanted more than that.

"How much do you know about the lifestyle?" he asked.

"More than you think." Her hand fluttered to her throat. Was she going to do this? Yes, it was time to jump into the deep end.

"We will need to discuss that, but for the moment, let's start off slowly and see how things go."

"What does that mean?" Slow? She already wanted to possess him and be possessed by him. Could she be patient enough to go slow?

Zeke blinked at her. "It means we're going to talk and talk some more. It also means being honest with each other and answering questions fully, holding nothing back."

She stiffened. "Do you think I've been lying?" Maybe this wasn't such a good idea.

"There you go. Jumping to conclusions. I see the tension in you. Why are you ready to run?" He kept his tone even and soft.

Allyson froze. Was she ready to run? Yes, and he'd noticed. Most men wouldn't. "Habit," she muttered, forcing her muscles to loosen. Wasn't that the truth?

"Can you talk about why it's a habit?" His fingers tightened around hers where their hands rested on her thigh.

"Maybe because my ex-boyfriends were jerks who never hung around, well, except the last one. I kicked him to the curb." Well, she certainly blurted that out. Allyson closed her eyes, not wanting to see Zeke's reaction.

"Allyson, honey, open your eyes, please."

She shook her head. Warm fingers cupped her chin, then the other hand released her fingers and slid around the back of her neck. "Maybe this will help. I've never had a lasting relationship either."

She peeked from under her lashes. "Oh?" She hadn't expected that from him. So he's a love 'em and leave 'em type of guy. Maybe they could have a fling.

"Yeah, I think my family scares them away." He released her chin.

"Your family?" Her lashes rose, and she stared at him. Could his family be scarier than hers? She doubted it.

"Yes. I have a younger brother and sister, remember." She nodded. "I love them to death, but they like to make a fuss when I bring someone to dinner with my parents. Well, right now it's just my sister, since my brother is military."

"Have you taken someone home for dinner

often?" A pang of longing hit lower in her belly. Her parents had all but abandoned her by the time she was twelve. She had to rely on herself for meals, getting her butt to school, almost everything.

"I've taken women home to meet my parents three times to be exact. I'm not a monk, but I don't take all the women I date home to meet the folks."

"Then why hasn't some woman snatched you up by now?" She clamped her hand over her mouth. What was it with Zeke that caused her to blurt out what she was thinking?

His laugher floated over her skin like soft breeze. "Because I haven't found the right woman yet."

Her eyebrows rose. "Really?" Somehow she couldn't see it.

"Yes, Miss Doubter." His fingers caressed the back of her neck. "So the exes were jerks. Did any of them hurt you?"

"What? No, nothing like that. No physical abuse." Why would he ask her that?

"There's more than physical."

True. She'd gotten enough verbal abuse from her parents to recognize it. "Agreed, but not with the ex-boyfriends." Nope, if they started that crap on her, she walked away and never looked back.

Zeke leaned back and released her as the waiter approached with the food. Did he have built-in radar to know someone was approaching them?

Several platters were placed on the table, and a wooden tray held sauces. Plates were set in front of them. "Please enjoy your dinner, and if you need anything at all, let me know."

"Thank you," Zeke said, and the waiter left.

Allyson's mouth watered at the smell of beef. "That smells heavenly." Her stomach rumbled, reminding her it had been a while since she'd eaten.

"Best barbecue I've found in the area." He picked up the tongs from the platter. "What would you like?" He held her plate in his other hand.

He was going to serve her? She opened her mouth to object, then stopped. Maybe this was what she'd been missing. A man who wanted to care for the woman he was dating. She wasn't used to being put first in a man's life. She looked over the platters. "A little bit of everything, please." She'd function better on a full stomach.

Zeke began to fill her plate. "I had them cook everything without any sauces so you can add your own."

"Thank you." She looked over the sauces and picked up the one labeled *sweet* and poured some on the side of her plate after Zeke set it in front of her. A shadow fell over the table.

"Forgive the interruption, I forgot to bring your rolls. These are fresh out of the oven." The waiter placed a basket on the table.

"Oh, that smell." Allyson didn't hesitate, she grabbed one of the rolls and pulled it apart. The fresh aroma made her tummy grumble.

"I love fresh bread too." Zeke grabbed two and put them on his plate, then loaded food onto the dish.

They both dug into their food. Allyson marveled

at the flavors exploding on her taste buds. The sweetness of the barbecue sauce along with the taste of perfectly cook beef brisket. The baby back rib meat fell right off the bone, and the pulled pork… She piled it onto one of the rolls and took a bite.

Her gaze caught the big grin on Zeke's face. She chewed and swallowed, then wiped her mouth with her napkin. "Do I have sauce on my face?"

"No. It's nice to see a woman enjoy a meal."

She ducked her head. "I like food."

"I'm glad you do." His voice was soft.

Allyson waited to see if he said more, but he didn't. She went back to her food. How refreshing it was to have a man who didn't frown at her when she ate more than a salad or a small piece of chicken. If there was one thing Allyson loved, it was food. She was lucky her job kept her out and busy so she didn't gain weight.

She finally pushed her plate away and held up her hands when Zeke tried to give her more. "I can't. I'm so full."

"So, no dessert?" He sounded disappointed.

"Give me a little bit and then we'll see." Right now, she'd explode if she ate more.

"Works for me." He waved the waiter over. "If you could split this up into two to-go boxes, please." Zeke glanced at her. "Another beer?"

"No, thank you. Some hot tea would be nice."

"One hot tea and one coffee please. We'll decide on dessert in a little bit."

"Perfect, sir. I'll box up your food and bring your

hot drinks." He whisked away the platters and their plates.

"Now that one appetite is satisfied, shall we work on the next one?"

"And what is that?"

"Knowledge." He shifted, and his thigh brushed hers. "How involved with kink have you been?"

Allyson swallowed and glanced around. No one near them. "I was active in the Seattle private party scene."

He whistled softly. "Private parties? For how long?"

"Several years." The parties helped her keep herself centered, and after some of the guys she'd dated, she needed an outlet.

"Why Seattle?" There was concern in his voice.

"You're worried. Why?"

"I've seen some of the Seattle scene; it's not exactly the best for a woman by herself."

"I can't argue with that." She couldn't. There had been times when she walked out of a party because she felt unsafe.

"Then I'll ask again: Why Seattle?"

Allyson glanced away from the concern in his eyes. How did she explain this? "I told you I wasn't into relationships."

"Due to the exes, yes."

"Well, in Seattle, the odds of running into someone from Pleasant Valley are slim, especially at the private play parties."

"What kind of play were you involved with?"

"Light bondage and…" She glanced away from Zeke. Why was this so hard for her? She'd talked to plenty of men at these parties about her preferences, and while a lot of the men weren't a fit for her, there were a few. She blew out a breath and glanced at Zeke. He was sitting patiently, waiting for her to answer. "Sometimes sex was involved." Her voice was soft.

"I see." Those brown eyes regarded her, not with anger or disdain, but with curiosity. "Let me ask you this question: How would you feel about kink without sex?"

She tilted her head. "It's fine. I didn't have sex with most of the men I played with at the parties." No, she'd been selective, about who she played with and who she had sex with. Sharing her body was a choice she didn't make lightly.

"For me, kink doesn't have to end in sex. Being in the lifestyle is about freedom you might not feel other places. About being able to let go of your inhibitions without worry or fear. To allow yourself to be you."

"I've never thought about it like that." She'd always kept a part of her tucked away when she played in Seattle. Another reason she left that behind her. She was becoming way too jaded, and she was too young for that. Allyson almost laughed out loud. Some thought thirty was old.

"Private play parties can have a much different vibe than a club like Wicked Sanctuary. It's one of the reasons I joined. I wanted more than sex or a hook up. I wanted to be able to relax and be myself."

"I can't see you any other way." It was the truth. Based on past experience—even as limited as it was—Zeke was the most patient Dom she'd ever met.

"You'd be surprised." He lightly stroked the hair at her nape.

A tremor went through her at his touch. "So are you saying no sex at the club?"

"Right. There are rules in place, and one of them is no sex in the club. That's not to say you won't experience the most amazing climaxes of your life under my hands."

Fire swept through her veins at his words. "I'm willing to try." She took a breath to steady herself. She wanted to explore with Zeke and discover his wants and needs in addition to her own.

"Outside of the private parties, have you done anything else? Read any books on the lifestyle?"

"I've read romance novels about the lifestyle." She looked down at the table as the waiter appeared with their drinks and to-go boxes. He set a teak box with a tea selection in front of her and left.

Allyson dug through the box and pulled out Darjeeling. This shouldn't keep her up all night, even if it was black tea. No, if she was sleepless tonight, it would be because of the man sitting next to her.

"Romance books are not bad places to get some information as long as it's done right."

"How would I know right from wrong in the books?" She was curious.

"Have you ever read a book and thought that it didn't seem realistic? Or maybe you wanted to bash the hero over the head because he was being an overbearing jerk? Maybe at a private party, you worried about a Dom who was being too rough?"

"Yes, there have been a few." Especially at the parties. It was part of the reason she stopped going. No, that wasn't completely true. She'd been questioning her actions for a while; the raid sealed it.

"I'm not going to say they're not doing it right. Everyone has their own idea of the lifestyle, and if it suits them, it's fine. But I'm with likeminded people who are seriously in the lifestyle, and it's not about abuse. It's about a power exchange. A give and take between Dom and sub."

"I've heard of the power exchange, but I don't fully understand. Isn't there always a give and take between Dom and sub?"

"Yes, but this is a connection that is both physical and mental."

Allyson thought about his words. "So you're not one of those overbearing men who expects me to obey his every word?" A shiver ran up her spine. She'd seen enough of those in Seattle and, after a few near-misses, stayed clear of them.

"I'm not. I like my sex kinky. I'm in charge in the bedroom, but I don't want to take over your life."

"That's a relief." She sagged in her chair.

"That's not to say I won't protect you."

"Like when you insisted on checking out my apartment before I entered."

"Right."

"I can live with that." She could. His

protectiveness actually made her feel cherished and safe.

"Have you used toys?"

This time she couldn't stop the heat that crept into her neck and face.

"Hmm, do I take your embarrassment as a yes?"

Allyson bit her lip. "Depends on what you mean by toys. A vibrator, yes. Not much else."

"That's fine. So you know your body and what arouses you."

She covered her face with her hands. "Can we talk about something else, please?" Why was she so embarrassed? Was it because they were in public?

His husky chuckle reached her ears. "There's nothing to be embarrassed or upset about. Most of us are sexual beings."

Allyson lowered her hands to find Zeke staring at her. His eyes held amusement. "True. But you said sex isn't the goal." She took a sip of her tea.

"Right."

"But it's always been mine." Well, crap. She'd blurted a private thought once again.

"Why is that?"

"Because that's what I know." Okay, her mouth was running away without her brain being engaged. She was telling Zeke things she never mentioned to anyone, except maybe Dani, but she'd known Dani since she was fourteen.

"Unacceptable." He shook his head. "Dessert?"

"No, I'm fine." She sipped her tea, wondering at the change of subject.

"Okay." Zeke motioned to the waiter. "Our check please."

"Of course, sir. Was the coffee not to your liking?" He motioned to Zeke's full cup.

"It's fine; we were just talking."

The waiter walked away, and Zeke picked up his cup and drained it. Allyson finished up her tea, recognizing that Zeke was, rather abruptly, ready to leave. "Do you have a problem with what I said?" she asked.

"Absolutely not. We need privacy for the rest of our conversation."

Private conversation. Oh boy, that could mean a lot. Allyson nodded as Zeke paid the bill, picked up their food, and escorted her back to his truck. The drive back to her place was quiet. Her body hummed with tension. Was Zeke going to walk away from her? It was possible. Her gut clenched at the thought of Zeke leaving her and then seeing him through work.

This is why she shouldn't date someone she worked with. When they broke up, because it would happen, how was she going to handle seeing him? Her heart clenched at the thought this might be their last date. She turned to him when he parked. "Thank you for dinner." Her voice wobbled as she reached for the door handle.

"We're not through, not by a long shot." He climbed out, made his way to her side, opened the door, and helped her out of his truck. After grabbing one of the bags of food, he waited while she opened the security door.

"Zeke, I understand." She put her hand on his forearm when they reached her apartment.

"No, you don't." He stared down at her. "Open the door and let me show you the difference between sex for sex's sake and sensuality."

"Bossy and arrogant." Why was her skin tingling from his words? Could it be hope he wasn't going to walk away? She opened the door and stepped inside. Zeke followed and closed the door behind him. "Maybe this isn't a good idea."

"It is. Let me put this in the fridge." He took the bag of food and went into the kitchen, then he was back. "I want you to look at your living room and describe what you see."

"Why? You can see it."

"An exercise."

Allyson shrugged her shoulders and glanced around her living room. It was nothing special. "There's a sofa with two side tables, a TV, pictures on the walls, a rug on the floor. It's small but homey."

"Is that all you see?"

"Yes." What did he expect her to say?

"Let me tell you what I see." He slipped his arms around her waist, bringing her back to rest against his chest. "I see a sofa with a crocheted blanket on the back. I suspect someone you respect made it for you. Lots of silk-covered pillows, which tells me you like the feel of soft luxury. The pictures on the walls. There's one that's a heart made out of wood, and through it, you see the ocean. There's another that is a silhouette of a couple standing at the water's edge at sunset in each other's arms. Oh, and the one of a woman wearing a mask. All sensual. It's not about sex; it's about emotions."

Her mouth dropped open. "I bought the pictures because I liked them. And the blanket..." Her gaze was drawn to it. "Dani's grandmother made that for me."

"And your bedroom. The purple and blue quilt on the bed, the sheets look soft and inviting. You have more pillows. The walls are painted a soft peach, and don't think I didn't notice the small pictures of a rose, a cowboy, the lips, and a couple entwined in each other's arms."

Damn, this man was observant. She'd forgotten those pictures were even there. "Why do you think that means I'm sensual rather than sexual?"

"Are you kidding me?" He shook his head. "It's in the way you walk, even in the way you dress. You pick colors that complement your skin, but also accent your body."

"What?" She started to pull away, but he tightened his hold on her.

"You don't do it on purpose. I bet you love the way soft material feels against your skin."

"I do." Again the words slipped from her mouth before she could stop them.

"Honey, I don't know who taught you that a relationship was all about sex, but it isn't. There is a deep sensuality to you, and it's going to take the right person to bring it out."

"And you think that's you?"

"As arrogant as this is going to sound, yes. Right now, you're in my arms and not tense but relaxed."

She was, and she hadn't even realized it. Allyson was comfortable with Zeke, and there weren't many men she could say that about. She squirmed in his hold. "Doesn't mean anything." Why was she being so stubborn around this? Maybe because she'd seen the way her parents acted when she was growing up, like sex was all there was to life. If Zeke walked, it would hurt much more than anyone she'd dated before. She already knew that.

"It does." He turned her in his arms. "Who scared you away from your sensuality?"

"Who says I'm scared?" She lifted her chin.

Zeke grinned. "There's my spunky lady." He rubbed his nose against hers, and her skin tingled at the contact.

"Now that we've got that out of the way…" She wanted to move the conversation in another direction.

"I know there's more you have yet to reveal," Zeke said. "I'll wait, for now."

"Thank goodness," she whispered, and he chuckled.

"But you need to understand I am a Dominant, and I'm a member of Wicked Sanctuary."

"Ummmm, right." Dani was a member. Had she seen Zeke there? And why didn't Dani warn her.

"And I believe you're a submissive."

"I am not."

"Do you feel comfortable taking the lead in the bedroom? Telling a man what to do?"

"In the bedroom, no. Outside of it, yes."

"Sexual submissive then."

"That's a new term for me."

"We'll discuss what all of it means on another night. I remember you said you had an early morning meeting. I want you to feel comfortable with me. Are you open to us going out again as more than friends?"

Allyson tipped her head back and stared at him. "Yes." She wasn't going to hold herself back, no matter how much it might hurt in the end. She deserved this. She wanted to be with Zeke, to see what they could do together. "I'd like us to go out again."

"Good. I'll give you a call tomorrow, and we'll set up our next date. Until then..." He cupped her chin as his lips covered hers.

She sighed into the kiss, enjoying the feel of his mouth against hers. The way his tongue dipped in and retreated. His body against hers. Oh yes, she was going to enjoy getting to know this man better.

When he lifted his head, she was out of breath. Zeke smiled at her. "Until tomorrow. Lock the door after me." He released her, unlocked the door, and left.

She lifted her fingers to her lips. They throbbed from his kiss. This was crazy. Scary crazy. Then again, maybe not. Locking the door, she made her way into her bedroom. Tomorrow, she'd talk with Dani. She needed to understand more about the lifestyle Zeke described.

* * * *

Thursday morning, Allyson sat in Wes's office, twisting her fingers together. This shouldn't be that hard of a conversation. She'd checked the HR regulations again. They were vague about personal relationships in the workplace.

"What did you need to talk to me about?" Wes asked.

Cards on the table. "There's no fraternization component to our HR regulations."

Wes sat up. "There's nothing in there about dating someone in the same department or even working for the city."

"Right, but this is outside of that. Wes, I'm starting a relationship with the owner of Riggs Construction. I don't want anyone to think I'm doing him any favors, so if it means taking me off of all his jobs, then that's what has to happen."

His eyes widened. "Let's talk about this. Because there's only you and Rudy doing the overall inspections, I can't afford to give Rudy all the Riggs Construction jobs. Would you mind if I got HR involved?"

"No, please do. I've read the regulations over and over and can't find anything."

Wes picked up his phone, and within a few minutes, Linda from HR walked into his office. "Is there a problem?" Linda asked after sitting down.

"There might be. I think not, but I need an HR perspective." Wes outlined what Allyson had told him.

"Hmmm, there's no real policy." Linda looked at

Allyson. "But it means when you're on the job there can be no slip ups. You cannot let your relationship interfere with your job. There can't even be a hint of anything other than business."

Allyson nodded. "We're only having dinner out right now, to see where things go."

Linda nodded. "Because the department is so small, I know lines blur, and there's no concrete rule. But keep the private life, private. By that I mean very private. On the job, there can be no doubt that there is no favoritism."

"I can do that. I don't believe in showing favor over one company to another, or one person to another when it comes to my job. People can be hurt if I mess up." Allyson took a breath.

"Good. Wes, any questions?" Linda asked.

"Nope. I wanted to make sure how HR felt about this."

Linda turned to Allyson once again. "Off the record, you're a model employee. Keep things out of the office, and everything will be fine."

"Thanks." Allyson's muscles relaxed.

"Then I'm done here." Linda stood and left.

"I agree with Linda's assessment and yours. You've never shown favoritism to anyone that I've noticed, especially not Riggs or Starr. You write them both up when things are not done correctly."

"I haven't had to write Riggs up for a while." She had in the beginning, mainly minor stuff. But just like the missing plug cover, she wrote it on her report; that was her job, and she took pride in it.

"You'll do fine. Was there anything else?"

"No. I wanted you to be aware." Allyson stood up and left. Well, that was out of the way, for now anyway. She would tell Zeke what was said. Life was about to get interesting.

* * * *

Allyson pulled up to Sweet and Savory on Friday with a smile. She needed this lunch with Dani. After seeing Zeke Wednesday, she needed to talk to her best friend. This morning, she'd found a box sitting on her desk.

Zeke. He must have forgotten to not send her any more gifts at work. She opened the box to see a miniature rose encased in glass. A beautiful paperweight. The note made her smile.

Last one at work, I promise. I saw this and knew you needed it. Z.

She put the paperweight on her desk. If anyone asked, she'd say it was from a friend. Rudy could make all the remarks he wanted.

A part of her was tickled pink that Zeke was being so thoughtful and attentive.

Dani already had a table, and Allyson waved to her as she entered. "Want me to get our lunch?" she offered as she set her bag on the empty chair.

"Sure. You know what I like," Dani said as she dug her wallet out.

"I'll get it."

"You got it last time." Dani handed her some cash. "Don't argue with me."

Allyson laughed and took the money. She took

her place in line, ordered, and was handed a number. Lara told her to put it at the end of her table, that they were trying something new.

"They're bringing the food to the table now?" Dani asked as Allyson placed the number at the end of the table and handed Dani her change.

"Looks like it. It makes sense with the café being so busy. This way, they don't have people stacked up waiting." Allyson noticed how the tables were full, and there were more employees than before. This was good for Lara and her business. And if Allyson remembered the timeline right, the wall between the café and the ice cream shop would come down this weekend.

"Movie tonight?" Allyson asked.

"I can't. I'm working," Dani said.

"How? You're working in the dark now?"

Dani giggled. "Sorry, I'm working at the club."

"Oh?" Allyson leaned forward. Ever since Zeke told her he was a member, she wanted to know more about Wicked Sanctuary. "What are you doing?"

Dani tilted her head and stared at her. "Checking people in, that's all."

Allyson looked up as their food was delivered. "Thank you." They both dug in, and after a few minutes, Allyson came up for air. That's what she got for skipping breakfast.

"So you're checking people into the club." Allyson had a thousand questions swirling around in her mind.

Dani polished off her sandwich. "Yes. I can see

you're curious, but I'm restricted in what I can tell you."

"I understand." She scrunched up her nose. Maybe that's why Dani hadn't told her Zeke was part of the club. She thought about how to phrase the question she wanted to ask. "Do you think I'm submissive?"

Dani choked.

Allyson started to stand, but Dani waved her back into her seat and grabbed a drink.

"Are you okay?" Allyson asked.

"Yes," Dani answered, her voice scratchy. "You sure know how to surprise a person."

"Sorry." Allyson glanced away. Maybe this was a bad idea.

"Don't be. A little warning would have been nice. What brought this on?"

Allyson shrugged. "I had dinner with Zeke the other night. There's a connection between us, and we talked a little bit."

"Ah, the beginning of the kink talk. Did you tell him about the parties in Seattle?"

"I did, and he told me there was so much more to kink than sex."

Dani grinned. "There is. I'm so glad you're listening to him."

"I'm trying, but I'm still unsure."

"Tell me more."

Allyson's tummy did a backflip. "As I said, we went out to dinner again Wednesday night, and Zeke was attentive, but also protective. We talked a little about kink. He told me he was a Dominant and that I was a submissive. When I questioned him on that, he said I was submissive in the bedroom." She paused and glanced around. "He also told me he belonged to Wicked Sanctuary."

"Goodness." Dani sat back in her chair. "What has you unsure?"

"I've never considered myself submissive. Yes, I like a man to take charge but only in certain situations."

"I get it." Dani leaned forward. "Being submissive is intensely personal."

"Am I being intrusive?"

"No, we've never talked about it in detail. You liked the private parties, but I didn't."

"Yet you go to Wicked Sanctuary."

"I do." Dani rubbed her nose. "How can I explain?"

"You own your own business. I've never seen you as submissive, even though you've told me you are. Is it only in the club?"

"Yes and no. What Zeke said about a bedroom submissive is pretty close to what I am. I found I enjoy letting a man have control in the bedroom, but only the bedroom."

"Okay." Allyson listened to Dani's words carefully trying to understand.

"When I experimented in college, there were certain aspects to the lifestyle that appealed to me."

"Like what?"

"For me, it's about being able to let go at the end

of the week. At Wicked Sanctuary, I can find a Dom who understands what I need. He allows me to let go of my job, my worries, everything as we play."

"I've never had that." Allyson had to admit that sounded blissful. "But does that mean you have no control at all?"

"I control everything." Dani smiled. "It's one of the things that people not in the lifestyle don't understand. I can say no to anyone or to anything anytime I want. I decide to whom and how much control I want to give up to my Dom."

"You negotiate? Don't you mean, the Dom negotiates?" At the parties, she rarely saw a sub negotiate, usually the Dom did all the talking, not the sub. That was why she'd picked Doms who were more interested in sex when she needed it. Or those who knew her limits and respected them.

"We both negotiate. It's a give and take, but there are rules in the club that are to be followed. And trust me, if they're not, there are consequences."

"I think I'm confused." She rubbed her forehead. "I've never encountered what you're describing."

"Consequences happen in the right circles. I wouldn't give up control if I didn't feel safe."

"The club makes you feel safe?"

"Oh yes. I've never felt unsafe there, even when I first joined." Dani ran her fingers over her cheek. "How much time do you have before you have to go back to work?"

"I took the afternoon off." She didn't want to worry about how long of a lunch she took with Dani.

"Good. I know a place we can go and get you some great information on the lifestyle."

"Oh?"

"Yes. And you've been there before." Allyson frowned, and Dani laughed. "Finish up lunch and we'll go."

"All right." They finished quickly, and Dani drove her van back to her small office, where Allyson picked her up. Dani gave her directions, and when Allyson saw the bookstore, she laughed. "Yes, of course I've been to Kleinman's before. You made me come with you to the opening of the bookstore."

"I did, but today, we're starting in the bookstore, then we'll move on the adult side." Dani jumped out of Allyson's truck. The note on the bookstore doors said to enter through Kleinman's, so Dani pulled her to the door and opened it.

Allyson wasn't sure. She'd never been inside an adult store before. She was pretty sure it was partly from a misplaced sense of embarrassment attached to her parents conduct when she was young.

"Hey, Destiny," Dani said as she entered. "This is my friend, Allyson. We're going to go look around in the bookstore and then come back in here."

"Sure," the young lady with purple hair said. "Be careful. I haven't had a chance to unload some of the new books yet, so there are boxes on the floor."

"Will do." Dani took Allyson by the arm and led her down the aisle and through the doorway into the bookstore.

Allyson relaxed. The bookstore she could handle.

Besides they'd already been here. Dani pulled her down three aisles until they stopped in the alternative lifestyle section. So many books. She'd thought the same thing when Zeke showed her around when the bookstore held its grand opening.

"Okay, let's start you off with some simple stuff, but also educational." Dani plucked a book off the shelf, moved to the next bookcase, pulled another one off, and then a third. "I also think some different romances are called for. I know you usually read on your e-reader, but let's start you off with a new series that depicts the lifestyle a little more realistically."

Allyson followed Dani as she moved into the romance section. She plucked two books off the shelf. "Come on." Dani made her way back into the adult store. Allyson paused in the doorway between the two stores and looked around.

There was lots of light and openness to the adult side, and her muscles relaxed. No dim lighting. She didn't see any dark corners or booths in the back with old men coming out of them. She wasn't expecting something this… What? Elegant. No, that wasn't quite the word, but close.

Dani was halfway down another aisle, and she looked back to Allyson. "Come on."

Allyson caught up with Dani, who was standing in front of a display of restraints. Allyson's heart skipped several beats.

"You've told me you like to be lightly restrained." Dani juggled the books in one arm and picked up a box. "This should work."

"I don't need restraints." What was Dani thinking?

"Think of them as research while you read." Dani headed for the register with Allyson trailing after her. She had to admit her heart sped up as she spied toys and other things as she made her way to the front of the store.

"All done?" Destiny asked.

"Yep." Dani placed everything on the counter. "You still the sole employee?"

"Yes." Destiny began ringing up the purchases. "Damon is interviewing employees for this side. I've got a couple lined up for the bookstore side."

"Great," Dani said.

"It will be nice once we can get the place staffed. And that's $85.92."

Allyson reached for her wallet.

"Nope. This is on me." Dani handed over her credit card.

"Dani," Allyson started to protest.

"I'm your friend." Dani put her credit card away, then took the bag. "See you around, Destiny." Dani took Allyson's hand and pulled her out of the shop.

"I should have paid for the stuff."

"A gift." Dani put the bag in the bench seat and climbed into Allyson's truck.

Allyson cocked one brow in response to Dani's declaration before driving Dani back to her office. When they arrived, Dani got out but stood with the passenger door open. "Start with the romances, and then read the intro to BDSM. When are you seeing

Zeke again?"

"Sunday. We're going to lunch." He'd called her earlier asking to see her Sunday.

"Good. Get through as much as you can by then. It will give you lots to talk about. Don't be afraid to ask him questions, Allyson. Communication is key." Dani grinned. "Call me if you need anything before you see Zeke."

With that, Dani slammed the door. Allyson drove to her apartment and carried the bag inside.

Why did she have a feeling she was about to enter a world different from anything she'd previously experienced or imagined?

Chapter 6

Zeke rubbed the back of his neck before he got out of his truck Sunday at Allyson's apartment complex. He'd just come from his parents' house. He could still hear his mother complaining he didn't eat enough breakfast.

He hadn't mentioned he had a date for lunch. His family could be a little overwhelming when it came to him dating anyone. He'd talked with Allyson yesterday and asked her if having lunch at his home was an issue. She'd paused and then consented.

Consent was important to him. In kink and in a relationship. His stomach churned as he made his way to the front door. Zeke paused and took a deep breath before pressing the button for her apartment. Why was he so nervous? It didn't make sense, but he was.

Her clean, sweet voice came over the speaker. "Yes?"

"It's Zeke."

The door buzzed. He pushed it open, making sure it closed before walking down the hallway to her apartment. The door opened the second he stopped in front of it.

"Hi." She had pulled her hair back with clips, exposing her luscious neck.

"Hi, yourself." He smiled, and his nerves settled. "You look amazing. Ready to go?"

"Yes." She patted her purse and stepped out. Zeke waited while she locked up, then they headed for his truck.

"Do you live in town?" Allyson asked when he pulled out of the parking lot.

"I do. Over on Jackson."

"That's a nice area."

"I like it." Zeke concentrated on traffic, not that there was that much on a Sunday. Would Allyson like his modest home?

He'd been lucky enough a few years ago to find the land had already been developed and all the utilities run, but no homes had been built. He inquired and found out the builder had gone out of business. He bid on a half-acre lot and bought it for a song.

Since he was in construction, he decided to build his home the way he wanted it. Gabriel drew up the plans and helped him, along with his crew, to construct it.

It hadn't taken them long to get the house done. Furnishing it was another thing. Zeke asked his baby sister to help him. She laughed and told him he was helpless with interiors.

What was nice about the area was that most of the homes stood on half-acre lots, so there was plenty of room between houses, plus lots of green.

He turned up his long driveway.

"Is that your house?" Allyson asked with a note of awe in her voice.

"Yes." Zeke was proud of his home. The stone columns that held up the covered entryway. The wraparound porch. The exterior was a façade made to look like wood, while the solar panels on the roof gleamed in the sunlight.

Zeke stopped his truck at the front door. He hopped out and then opened Allyson's door.

"This is beautiful, Zeke." Her head turned from left to right, to left again. "Did you build it?"

"Guilty."

She smiled at him. "You're a talented man."

Zeke bit back a laugh. She had no idea of how talented he could be. That was the purpose of today, if she was willing. "Come on. Let's go in, and I'll give you a quick tour." Taking her hand, he led her up the steps to the front door.

He unlocked it and pushed it open. "Welcome to my home." He stepped aside and followed her into the foyer. After shutting the door, he slipped off his shoes and put them in the bin behind the door. She pulled her phone out of her purse and put it in the pocket of her jeans, before tossing her purse in with his shoes.

"Should I take mine off?" she asked.

"If you're comfortable doing so." He didn't force his guests to remove their shoes, but most did. Allyson toed off her sneakers and placed them in the bin.

"It's so bright and open," she said.

"I wanted a home full of light." He gestured to the right. "This is my small home office." A desk with his laptop sat against the wall. A drafting table in front of the window. He took a few steps. "This is the family room."

Her eyes grew wide. "I love all the windows." She moved farther into the room and ran her fingers over the back of the light gray sectional as she walked over to the glass doors that led to the patio.

"To your left, you'll see the kitchen and the dining room." He glanced over to make sure he'd cleared off the breakfast bar before he left this morning. He had a tendency to leave stuff piled on it. Oh good, he had cleaned it off.

"How many bedrooms?" she asked as she looked out at the covered deck.

He joined her. "There's the master suite and a guest bedroom." He followed her gaze as she looked out. His yard was looking good. Since it was getting into May, and the weather was warming up, it was coming back to life after the cold, rainy winter.

"May I?" she gestured to the door.

"Be my guest."

She unlocked the door and pushed it open, then walked out onto the teak deck. He was glad it was nice today. "Would you like to eat out here?"

Her blue eyes lit up. "If you don't mind." She sighed. "It's so nice to be outside when we have sun. This is one of things I miss being in an apartment: having a yard where I can sit and be one with nature."

"Then we'll eat out here. But first…" Zeke walked over to the wall and flipped a couple of switches. The full-height glass doors that enclosed the deck retracted.

"Oh my goodness."

"A nifty feature when I want fresh air, but it keeps the bugs away when I sit out here at night and dry during winter." Zeke pulled out one of the wicker chairs. "Come sit down and enjoy the view while I get our lunch."

"Do you want some help?"

"No." He patted the cushion on the back of the chair. "I'll take care of everything."

After a slight hesitation, Allyson sat in the chair he held. "This is absolutely beautiful, Zeke."

He leaned down and took a deep breath. She smelled of vanilla and spring. His cock stiffened. "I'm glad you like it. Be back in a few minutes with food and drink." He slipped back into the house. In the kitchen, he gripped the counter. He'd almost kissed her back there. Not that it would be a bad thing, but there were things they needed to discuss first.

That was the purpose of today. To get to know each other better and to discuss kink in private. Allyson's knowledge of the lifestyle was from private play parties; he wanted her to know there was so much more to kink than the parties.

* * * *

Allyson stared out into Zeke's expansive back yard. She could sit here for hours doing nothing. This was her idea of heaven. Her phone beeped, and she pulled it out of her pocket.

Dani: *Have you talked with Zeke yet?*

Allyson grinned at her friend's text message.

Allyson: *Not yet, just got to his house. He's getting us lunch now.*

Dani: *How do you like his house?*

Allyson: *It's beautiful. Wait…have you been here?*

Dani: *Who do you think did the landscaping.*

Lots of smiling emojis followed Dani's words.

Allyson: *All right. Point taken.*

Dani: *Remember what I told you last night, and you'll be fine. Have fun.*

Allyson turned her phone off and slipped it back into her pocket as butterflies tumbled around in her stomach. She'd called Dani last night after she finished the intro to BDSM book. Luckily, Dani had been on a break at the club and could talk.

Zeke came back out to the deck with his hands full. Allyson jumped up. "Let me help you." She took the platter of finger sandwiches from him.

"Thank you." He placed three bowls of chips on the table.

"Is there someone else joining us?" She looked at all the food on the table. Not only the sandwiches and chips, but fruit, crackers, and cheese.

"Nope, just us. Be right back with plates and drinks."

Allyson shook her head. "Did you think you were feeding an army?" She stood by the patio doors, watching him in the kitchen. She loved the open floor plan.

"I wasn't sure what you liked." He picked up plates, placemats, napkins, utensils, and then a small cooler that looked like it could hold a twelve pack of cans.

"I'm not a super picky eater." She took the plates, placemats, and napkins from him. She put the placemats down first, then the plates, and set the napkins in the middle.

"Thank you." He placed the utensils on the placemats and set the cooler on the table and opened it. "I have water, soda, and beer. Name your poison."

"Water for right now." She sat down and stared at the food. Her stomach growled.

He grinned. "Don't be shy. Dig in."

Allyson took several different sandwiches and put them on her plate, then scooped up some chips. She'd do fruit and cheese later. Zeke waited until she was done before he took food for himself.

The patio was quiet as they ate. "These sandwiches are delicious. But I have to ask what they are?" She got hints of flavors but couldn't quite figure them out.

"There are three kinds as you've probably noticed. Right in front of you, is turkey salad, made with cranberries, mayo, mustard, and a hint of sage. Next to them on the right, is chicken salad, mayo, mustard, celery, a hint of onion, and pecans. The last is a tuna salad, mayo, celery, and pickle relish."

"I would have never thought about adding pecans or pickle relish." Those were giving the sandwiches a little extra kick.

"It gives them a little more flavor."

"How did you come up with it?"

Zeke grinned. "I didn't. Damon is a good cook. I called him and asked him what to do. Most of what he gave me was stuff way beyond my expertise level, so we settled on these."

"They are great. Why the different bowls of potato chips?" There were plain, barbecue, and corn chips.

"I wasn't sure what you'd like."

"For the record, any of them are fine."

"Noted." He pushed his plate aside and pulled out a bottle of water from the cooler. "More water or something else?"

"Diet soda, if you have it."

"I do." He pulled one out and opened the can for her. "I should go get you a glass." He set the can down and stood.

"Nonsense." She snatched the can. "I'm fine." Allyson took a drink. Zeke was still standing, staring at her. "Sit down, Zeke. Haven't you ever seen a woman drink out of can before?" His bemused expression made her smile.

"No, unless it's family."

She laughed. "I don't need a glass to enjoy a soda. Besides, we're friends having a nice casual lunch."

"Yes, we're friends." His heart warmed at his words. He took a long drink of his water. "Since we're beginning to head beyond friendship boundaries, are you ready to discuss a few things?"

Allyson swallowed. "I guess." Her gaze went to

the table.

"If you're not ready, I can wait."

"No." The word burst from her. Allyson took a calming breath. "I think we need to have this talk, especially since we're going to go beyond friendship." She took another sip of her soda. "I should tell you that Dani and I talked Friday over lunch."

"Oh?" His eyebrows rose.

"Nothing to worry about. I know Dani is a member of Wicked Sanctuary, but she didn't tell me anything she shouldn't. I needed to talk with someone after our dinner out and what you told me."

"Did I scare you?"

"Excited me was more like it." Communication, truthful communication, Dani told her, as did the book she read. "I've always felt that sex was more important than a relationship."

Zeke opened his mouth, and she held her hand up. She needed to get this out. "Zeke, I know what you showed me. When I was growing up, all my parents seemed to care about was sex. They never really had a relationship, even though they were married. So that's how I thought my life should be." She wasn't going to mention how her parents were swingers, not right now. "So, to me, sex was an itch to scratch, and after a while, I didn't like how that felt. I stopped going to the parties in Seattle after one was raided. It didn't feel safe anymore." Her hand fluttered to her chest. "Dani and I talked a bit about this. She found me a few books to read to help me better understand the lifestyle you described."

"What kind of books?" He kept his gaze on her but didn't seem upset by what she was saying. She blew out a breath, and her muscles relaxed.

"A couple of romances, an introduction to BDSM, and another book on the Dom/sub relationship."

"Can I ask where you got the books?"

"Kleinman's bookstore. Dani took me there Friday, and she picked them out." She didn't tell him about the restraints. She was still coming to terms with owning them.

He nodded. "Good choice. Dani would know what would be the best for you and what to start with."

"Yeah, well…" She ducked her head. Why was she embarrassed? She wasn't a virgin by any means, but she felt a little out of her depth here. "The romance was a little different than I've read before."

"How?" His voice was quiet.

"More intense, more into the lifestyle."

"Did you like it?"

"I did. Then I started on the introduction to BDSM book." Boy was that eye opening.

"It scared you?"

"Yes and no." She took another sip of her soda. "This is hard for me."

"I'm proud of you for trying. Why was it hard for you?"

"Because…" Allyson looked away. How did she explain? With honesty and open communication. "Zeke, I'm not used to talking about my emotions or about my needs."

"You said your parents put an emphasis on sex and not a relationship."

"Right. They weren't faithful to each other." Or at least that's how she saw it. Now she understood more.

Zeke swore, and Allyson stared at him with her mouth open. "I'm sorry. No kid should know that about their parents. Did they ever divorce?"

"No. I won't say there weren't fights, but for some reason, they stuck together."

He nodded. "Thank you for sharing with me."

"I was lucky I met Dani when I was fourteen." Her lips turned up.

"You've been friends a long time."

"Yes. She was the one who got past my tough kid persona because the other kids would tease me about my parents." Rumors traveled fast in the area where she grew up in Pleasant Valley. "We became fast friends. I spent a lot of time with Dani and her grandparents."

"I'm glad you had someone."

"Yeah. Once I turned eighteen, I left home. Dani's grandparents let me rent a room, and I went to work and took night classes at the college."

"How long did you live with Dani's grandparents?"

"A little over a year. I worked two jobs, studied, and saved everything I could. Dani's grandmother would feed me and refused to let me pay for food." She turned her hand over in his. "Once I was able to move out and get a better job, I was able to take more than one night class a semester, but I never forgot what Dani's grandparents did for me. I still send them things like fruit of the month or other things to repay their kindness."

"Probably the first genuine warmth you'd had in a while."

"Yeah." She hadn't thought about it that way, but Zeke was right. Dani's grandparents treated her like she was special not a burden.

"If I remember right, you said you took classes in Urban Planning and Development?"

Allyson's muscles relaxed in relief. He wasn't going to question her anymore about her childhood. "I was taking night classes, trying to figure out what I wanted to do with my life." Her gaze met his. "I kind of fell into it. There was a job fair, and one of the places hiring was the city. I started off in the Building and Code Enforcement department and worked my way through the system in various jobs. My current boss, Wes, hired me in the planning division to handle the front counter."

"He noticed your problem-solving talent."

Her jaw dropped open. "How did you know that?"

"I've watched you for a long time. You're good at figuring things out. There are times when I can almost see you working the problem out in your head."

Allyson bit her lip, then continued. "Wes took me under his wing and mentored me until I was able to become a full inspector."

"You enjoy your job."

"I do. It's fun. I'm not always behind a desk, and like you said, I like solving problems."

"Good. You mentioned some ex-boyfriends. How long were you in relationships with them?"

She scrunched up her nose. "Nothing beyond a few months, but they weren't relationships."

"Okay, I've had a few over the past years, but nothing special. Now, here's the explosive question: What do you think about the lifestyle?"

Allyson met his gaze. There was a little bit of worry there, not that she blamed him. "From my reading, it's different from what I thought." She glanced out at the trees, trying to gather her thoughts. "After reading the new romance books and the BDSM book Dani got me, I can see there is so much more to the lifestyle than what I was exposed to at play parties in Seattle."

He nodded. "Learning from books can be good. Just so you feel safe with the person you decide to play with."

"I feel safe with you." It was true. She wouldn't be in his home talking to him like this if she didn't. Had she truly felt safe with guys at the parties in Seattle? Nope. Not completely, which was why she had set up a safety system with Dani when she went.

"I'm glad you trust me."

"How did you get into the lifestyle?" She was curious about him.

"I was eighteen, and while I had a solid upbringing, I wasn't centered in life."

When he finished telling her how he got into the

lifestyle, she asked, "Tell me about your family." She craved stories about families that were closer to what she saw on TV or read in books.

"My parents are typical. They have a home in the Laurel neighborhood. And I told you about my younger sister and brother. My brother is in the military, and my sister is studying to become a doctor."

"Have you always had your own company?"

"No." His features tightened. "I used to work for Starr Construction."

"I feel like I should say I'm sorry." The jobs she'd gotten with Starr were always a fight to get them to do things according to code.

"Let's just say it was never a good fit. I started Riggs Construction four years ago, and I'm glad I did." He took a deep breath. "I told you about my management degree in civil engineer construction, but I also got one in business management."

"That's a big load."

"I was up for the challenge."

"Somehow I think you were." She watched his face as he spoke. He enjoyed what he was doing and was proud of his business, as he should be.

"Anyway, in college I was still a bit unsettled. I found a class on rope bondage."

"They taught bondage at college?"

"Not at the school. It wasn't called that, but that's what it was. It was being given at a local community center. Members of the local kink community were giving the class."

"And you enjoyed the class?"

"Very much so. It's amazing what it does for my focus. When I came back to Pleasant Valley, I had a new skill."

"Wait a second, you aren't much older than I am, and Wicked Sanctuary didn't open until five years ago."

"That's when Max opened the club, yes, but there was a pretty good size kink community in Pleasant Valley even before then."

He smiled, and to Allyson, there was a touch of wicked in the way his lips quirked up. Shivers raced up her spine at his intense gaze.

"Turns out, I have an affinity for tying knots."

"I bet." She grinned at him; he'd had her emotions tied in knots for a long time now.

"I met more people in the community, and one of the Doms took me under his wing, taught me about the lifestyle and what it meant to be a Dom." His gaze turned unfocused as he remembered. "It was a good time, and it helped me."

"How did it help?" This was so different from what her parents had and the play parties in Seattle.

"It helped me focus and kept me centered. I'd always been a bouncy kid. My parents had me tested for everything, but I was one of those high energy kids."

"You always seem to have a lot of energy."

"Yes, I do have to be careful, because I will crash after a while, so now I make sure I'm sleeping and eating properly." He kept his gaze on her. "Have you dabbled in kink besides light bondage?"

"No, but I am curious." After going to Kleinman's Friday and reading the books, her curiosity had spiked further. Dani had been really helpful when they talked.

"We'll start slow."

Allyson sighed. She wasn't sure she wanted to go slow. "How slow?"

"Questioning me already?" There was laughter in his voice, but that didn't stop Allyson from ducking her head. Then she raised it back up. She had nothing to be worried about. This was Zeke, and they weren't in play mode. "Hey." He waited until their gazes connected once again. "You can ask anything, and I mean that."

"You won't get upset if I question you about something you're doing?"

"I won't. In the BDSM book you read, did it talk about the Dom/sub relationship?"

"Yes." That was something she was very interested in. A man to take over in the bedroom. She was all for that.

"Did it also talk about the Master/slave relationship?"

"A bit, but not in detail."

"All right. I'm into the Dom/sub relationship. While there are some rules and protocols, we decide on them together. We're a team. The Dom/sub relationship for me is in the bedroom and at Wicked Sanctuary…if you decide you wish to play there."

"I'd like that."

"I'll still be protective outside the bedroom, but I won't tell you what to do or anything like that. Unless I think you're in danger."

"I get it." She did. From what she read, it seemed like a lot of Dominants were protective of their partners.

"The first thing I want to talk about is consent. I will ask for consent before I do anything we haven't discussed before, and we will have safe words."

"I read about safe words."

"Did you not have them at the play parties?"

"No, but then again, I was never alone with someone I'd just met."

Anger flared in his eyes, and he gripped the arms of his chair. She sat back. Had she made him angry with her? Maybe this wasn't a good idea.

"Sweetheart." Zeke's voice was soft and gentle. "My anger isn't directed at you, but at those who ran the parties and the people they let in."

"Why?"

"The one thing that was drummed into me was consent and safe words, and that's how Max operates the club. We believe in Safe, Sane, and Consensual."

"I read about that." She looked away from Zeke and out into his yard. "It wasn't very safe or sane at those parties; I see that now. I'm not even sure how much consent there was." She turned to him. "But I will tell you that, for me, there was always consent between me and my partner."

"Good. I'm glad you didn't allow anyone to talk you into something you didn't want to do."

Her lips turned up. "You know me fairly well by now. Can you really see someone talking me into something I don't want to do?"

Zeke laughed. "Maybe Dani."

"Yeah, she could." Her heart lightened at his laughter.

"All right, so we abide by SSC rules. The lifestyle has been around for a long time. It's coming more and more into the limelight, and people are starting to be more accepting."

"It does seem like more people have gotten involved."

"Yes. So we use safe words like red for stop, yellow for slow down, and green for keeping going."

"Doesn't it get frustrating using safe words all the time?"

"No. After a while, a couple playing together understands each other's rhythm, and the Dom learns to read his sub's non-verbal cues."

"You can do that?" She never thought about that.

"Yes. Like right now, you're sitting back in your chair, so your either testing what I'm saying or you're getting more comfortable."

Allyson giggled. She hadn't expected that. "I was getting more comfortable." This was fascinating to her, and maybe a little scary that he could read her so easily. "So now what?"

"What kind of kink you want to explore? What you don't want. Your hard limits."

The book on intro to BDSM talked a bit about these subjects, and as she read, it became clear how little she truly understood about BDSM in general. "I don't know what I'd like or not like in a kinky relationship."

"Which is why we talk."

"Isn't there another way? If we talk everything out, it will take forever."

"Impatient to jump right in?"

"I am."

"I'm glad. I was worried you'd run out screaming, but I don't want you to get scared or hurt, so we're going to do this my way. You're a novice. Can you agree to that?"

His tone dropped to a husky firm tone that sent shivers of awareness over her skin. "I can try, but I can't guarantee I won't get impatient."

"I get that. If you feel I'm moving too slow, talk with me. That's one of the most important elements – we keep the lines of communication open and honest."

"Dani explained that to me."

"We need to go over your likes and dislikes and limits. I know an easy way, if you're okay with me calling Max and asking for the club questionnaire."

"Sure." Why not? Once she went to the club with Zeke, others in the club would know, so filling out the questionnaire now wasn't such a big deal.

"Thank you. Be right back." Zeke stood and walked down the step to the yard before pulling out his cell phone.

Allyson kept her gaze on him as he talked. What was it about Zeke that pulled her to him? Yes, she liked him, but it was more than that. She was attracted to him, but she wanted more. Though his kisses were anything but simple. Heat filled her just thinking about them.

She thought back to the books she'd read over the last two days and couldn't deny the zing of excitement that went through her nerves when she thought about exploring with Zeke.

Zeke jogged up the stairs to her. "Max is emailing me the questionnaire. Give me ten minutes to pull it up and print it."

"Not a problem. Would you like me to put the food away?"

"I'll do it, but let's leave the chips out. Plus, I have dessert when you're ready."

"A man of many talents."

"I'd love to say I am, but I picked the desert up from Lara's café yesterday before she closed." Zeke picked up the plate of sandwiches. "Relax and enjoy the view." He strode into the house.

* * * *

Zeke put the sandwiches away and then fired up his computer. Within minutes he had the questionnaire printed out. How did he want to do this?

It would be better if they were inside, sitting close together, but outside could still work. The way the house was situated on the lot ensured privacy. He'd check to see how Allyson felt about being outside. Grabbing a pen, he set it and the questionnaire on the breakfast bar.

When he walked outside, Allyson was sitting on the double wide lounger. She looked comfortable. Maybe that was a better idea. He slipped inside, grabbed a clipboard, the pen, and paperwork.

Allyson glanced over at him and started to rise as he walked toward her. "No, stay there," he said. "Do you want something more to drink?" He noticed the side tables were empty.

"Water please."

Zeke grabbed two bottles out of the cooler and walked over to where Allyson reclined. He handed her one and set his on the side table before taking a seat. "We might as well be comfortable while we do this." Being outside in the fresh air was better, and it would keep him on his best behavior.

"This questionnaire is pretty in-depth, so ask me any questions you want."

"All right."

"I should also warn you it's alphabetical."

Allyson tilted her head and looked at him. "What do you mean?"

"For example: Anal sex is first. Is that something you're interested in?" Her cheeks flushed, and Zeke bit back a grin.

"No."

"So I'll put that as a hard limit." He checked the box.

"I want to make sure I understand correctly," Allyson interjected. "Hard limit is *no, never*, and a soft limit is *it's okay*?"

"You're right about any hard limit. On a soft limit,

you might like to try, maybe you're a little nervous, so we'll discuss it first. Let's say, nipple clamps. You'd like to try, but you don't want to be in pain. I would start you in something that wouldn't cause you pain, then as we play for a while, I might push that limit. But I would always talk with you about pushing the limit to let you know."

"And if I say my safe word?"

"If you say *red* the scene stops, and we go off and talk about it. If you say yellow, then I'll stop what I'm doing, and we'll talk to see if we want to continue the scene and the action or not."

"Okay, I think I got it."

"Let's look at the next item." Zeke continued down the list. He'd forgotten how extensive it was. They took several breaks, especially when he noticed Allyson was getting overwhelmed. When they got to the Rs, he stopped.

"Why don't you take this home and fill out the rest."

"There's so much." She ran her hand over her forehead.

"It is detailed, but it's good." They'd already gone over bondage, and he was pleased to see they matched up quite well in that area. "How are you feeling about all this?"

He'd checked in with her several times, and each time she said she was fine. Her body language spoke of a little bit of embarrassment and being uncomfortable, but she continued with her answers and asked him questions when she needed clarification.

"More detailed than I thought it would be." She slid off the lounger and stood. Allyson stretched her arms over her head, her breasts straining against her shirt, and his cock twitched.

Zeke turned away so he could adjust himself, then he picked up their empty drink bottles and made his way to the patio table. He'd taken the chips inside a while back. They'd eaten dessert while they went over the questionnaire.

"What time is it?" she asked, pulling her cell out of her pocket and turning it on. "Oh my goodness, it's almost five."

"Is it?" He glanced out at the yard. It was still light, but it was May, and the days were getting longer. "I hope I'm not making you late for anything."

"No. I didn't realize we'd taken that long." She preceded him into the house and made her way to the front door. "I did enjoy today." She pulled her purse and shoes out of the box and placed her purse on the bench beside her while she slipped her shoes on.

Once she was finished, Zeke took her hand. "I'm going to kiss you now."

"Please." She turned her face up to his.

He didn't hesitate and lowered his head. Her lips parted, and his tongue slipped inside, teasing and tasting her unique flavor. Arms slid around his waist as he cradled her close to him.

Allyson was special to him in a way he hadn't realized before. Her tongue brushed over his before retreating. His arms tightened around her waist, holding her closer to him.

Her hips shifted, making his cock pulse with need. He wanted her. Yes, he did.

In his arms.

In his bed.

In his ropes.

How would she look all trussed up with his knots accenting her beautiful body? Her skin pink, her breathing shallow, and her eyes filled with excitement and need.

His lips trailed from hers to her jaw and to her neck. "You smell so good." Vanilla and sunshine filled his senses.

"You feel so good against me." Her words were soft. "I haven't been with a man for a while."

"How long is that?" He slipped his palms to her butt and caressed them through the denim fabric.

"Six months."

"I see." He nipped at her throat, raising goosebumps over her flesh. He shifted, and his dick pressed harder against his jeans.

Her hand slid over his shoulders, and her fingers played with his hair.

Zeke couldn't help himself. He captured her lips with his as he pulled her closer, his cock pulsing.

Allyson's tongue tangled with his, drawing it into her mouth as she pressed closer to him, her breasts against his chest. Zeke groaned as she pressed a hand between their bodies and cupped his cock.

Damn! This woman could turn him on faster than a light switch. He wanted more. Breaking off the kiss, he cupped her breasts through her shirt. "So soft."

"So hard," she whispered, squeezing his dick.

Fuck. He wanted to pick her up and carry her into his bedroom right now. Need and want coursed through him. But first things first. "If we don't stop, I won't want to."

"I'm okay with that." Her eyes were slumberous with desire.

"That's not a step we're ready for yet." It wasn't. They were just getting to know each other and their limits.

Allyson sighed. "I guess you're right." Her arms slid from around his waist, and she took a step away from him. She pressed her hands to her cheeks while he wiped his hands over his face. They both needed to regain their composure.

"Dinner Tuesday?" His voice shook. Not exactly as in control as he wanted.

She lowered her hands and took a deep breath. "I'd like that." She picked up her purse.

"Would you mind eating here again? We can finish up the discussion on the questionnaire and go from there." With each breath, his control was coming back.

"I can do that. What time should I be here?" While the color was still high in her face, her voice was steady and calm. That was his Allyson.

"I'll pick you up." Zeke slipped on his boots and picked up his keys.

"Zeke, I can drive myself. It seems silly for you to pick me up to drive me back home later."

"I know you can, but I like being able to do little things for you." He opened the door to his truck.

"I've noticed." She flashed him a grin as he pulled out of his driveway. The ride was quiet. Zeke was lost in his thoughts. The way Allyson felt in his arms, her response to his kisses. He couldn't wait until they could play together. It would be explosive. When they arrived at her apartment, he walked her inside.

"This is something I'll have to get used to, isn't it?" she asked after he checked out her apartment.

"Yes." He drew her to him. "I will make sure you're safe."

She released a contented sigh as she rested her hands on his chest. "Have a good rest of your evening."

"You too." He brushed his lips over hers, not allowing the kiss to go too far before he guided her into her apartment, then walked out and closed the door behind him. He waited until he heard the snick of the deadbolt, then he sauntered to his vehicle. How could he be so lucky to hit the jackpot with Allyson? He didn't know, but he wasn't about to let her slip through his fingers. Not this time.

Tuesday night would be fun. He'd have to ask Allyson tomorrow if pizza was okay. His cooking skills were passable, but he'd rather spend time with her than cooking.

* * * *

Allyson found herself at Zeke's home again Tuesday evening. She'd finished going over the questionnaire with some help from Dani. They had a girls' night last night. Dani told her the questionnaire was part of the membership to the club, so it was great that Max allowed Zeke to use it, and if Allyson decided to join the club, she had half of the paperwork done.

She parked her small truck behind his big one. He'd called her earlier. He was out on a job in the opposite direction from her apartment and asked if she'd drive out. Zeke was so thoughtful, and while she appreciated it, she also wanted him to realize he didn't need to drive her all the time. She grabbed her bag, which held her purse and the questionnaire, and stepped out of her truck. A slight breeze brushed over her skin. Soon they'd be in full-fledged summer.

Zeke stood in the open doorway of his home with a smile. "Hi."

"Hey." The jeans he wore rode low on his hips and molded to his strong thighs. Allyson pressed her lips together so she wouldn't drool over him. The last few nights, her dreams had been filled with Zeke and all the wicked things he could do to her body.

"I'm glad you're here." Zeke leaned down and brushed a light kiss over her lips.

"Me too." She stepped inside, put her bag down, and was starting to remove her shoes when another vehicle pulled up. "Expecting someone else?"

"No." A frown marred his forehead.

A small woman slid out of the car. Her long black hair was caught back into a ponytail, and sunglasses covered her eyes. She all but bounced up the walkway.

"Hey, big brother." She enveloped Zeke in a hug that seemed larger than life.

So this was Zeke's younger sister. Allyson smiled at her exuberant greeting, yet a ball of nervousness swelled in her belly.

"What are you doing here, Josie?"

"I—" She broke off when her gaze met Allyson's. "Oh I'm sorry. You have company." Her gaze swept over Allyson from head to toe, then back to stare at Zeke. "It's about time."

Zeke shifted from one foot to the other with a pained expression. Allyson couldn't hold back a grin. "I'm Allyson." She held out her hand.

"Josie." They shook hands. "Sorry to interrupt."

"Right." Zeke drew his hand through his short black hair.

"I really need your help." Josie flipped off her sunglasses and stared up at her brother. Allyson almost laughed at the pleading look in her eyes. Is that what baby sisters did?

"What have you done this time?" Zeke stepped back, and Josie stepped inside, where she removed her shoes without prompting.

"It wasn't my fault." Josie glanced at Allyson. "It really wasn't, but Mom and Dad aren't happy."

Zeke sighed.

"Maybe I should go?" This was something between family members. It wasn't her place to be here. She was sure she had no clue how to deal with Josie or her problems.

"No." Zeke pinned Allyson with his gaze. "Josie,

go into the family room. We'll be there in a minute."

"Thanks, brother." Josie didn't seem bothered by her brother barking orders at her and took off in the direction of the family room. She must be used to her brother doing that.

"Zeke, we can do this another night." Allyson didn't want to get in the middle of a family issue.

"It shouldn't take me long to sort this out."

"Your sister needs you." Allyson slipped her foot back into the one shoe she'd slipped off. "Take care of her. We have time." She went up on her toes and brushed a kiss over his lips. "Call me tomorrow, and we'll set up another night."

"Tomorrow night. Same time, same place," Zeke said, clearly unhappy she was leaving.

"I can do that." She opened the door and left before Zeke could say more. Her stomach was already doing summersaults. Until she met Dani, she'd never been close enough to anyone when she was younger to be able to go to them when her family life went crazy.

Josie had parked on the other side of the driveway, so Allyson backed out easily. She'd grab some food on the way home. A tremor went through her body. This wasn't good. If she was uncomfortable with his sister, how would it be with the rest of his family? How could she have a true relationship with Zeke? Her gut clenched. It would take time, she reminded herself. Building blocks. It would get easier. At least she hoped it would. But the feelings of inadequacy plagued her.

* * * *

"Okay, spill," Zeke said to his sister when he walked into the family room. He couldn't be mad at Josie. He was aware that sometimes their parents put too much pressure on her.

"Allyson sounded nice. Why didn't she stay? Did I frighten her away?"

"She is nice, and she didn't stay because she felt this was a family issue, and she isn't family." Yet. Whoa, where did that thought come from? It was much too early to be thinking that way.

Zeke sat in his favorite chair and stared at his sister. "Tell me what's going on."

Josie waved her hand in the air. "I will. Let's have lunch together this week and invite Allyson. I'd like to get to know her better."

Zeke barely prevented himself from rolling his eyes. "You're already going to report back to Mom about her, so let's not compound the injury." It was going to be bad enough without an additional lunch. His parents would be on the phone wanting to meet Allyson the second his sister told them. This was why he hadn't dated very much. "Now tell me what brought you out here."

"I'm kind of flunking out of organic chemistry."

Zeke sat back in his chair. "Kind of?"

"Well, maybe actually."

"Flunking?" This wasn't like his sister at all. "What's going on, Josie?"

"I'm not sure. I get all the concepts, but when I go to the labs, I screw up."

"Have you talked to your instructor?"

"Yes. But I have to pass this class for my pre-med. I don't know what to do."

Zeke rubbed his chin. His knowledge of chemistry was limited. "What can I do to help?"

"You know so many people, do you know anyone who can help me? All the usual tutors are already booked up."

Zeke ran everyone he knew through his head. Dani might know a person. He heard her mention one time that she'd taken soil chemistry. "I know someone to talk to. I'll see if she knows anyone, but I can't guarantee anything. Make sure to keep working the tutor end."

"I am." She jumped up, ran over to him, and hugged him. "Thank you. Will you talk to Mom and Dad, too?"

"Yes." He chuckled.

"You're the greatest big brother. Dad threatened to make me move back home."

No wonder Josie was so concerned. She shared an apartment with two other university students who were also her best friends. While she could commute to her classes, it was a good drive from Pleasant Valley to the university outside of Seattle.

"I'm your only big brother. Ben is younger than you."

"Don't remind me." She straightened as the doorbell rang.

"Dinner." He'd forgotten about the pizza. "Want to stay? I got pizza."

"I never say no to pizza."

Zeke ruffled her hair on his way to the door. He'd spend some time catching up with his sister and then check in on Allyson.

* * * *

Wednesday afternoon, Allyson sat down at a table at Sweet and Savory. Zeke had asked her if she could meet him here, and she'd agreed. She needed a break from the office. Rudy was being obnoxious today. Maybe because she'd gone out to a Starr Construction site today and ripped them a new one.

Allyson glanced up as the chair across from her was pulled out, but it was Zeke's sister, Josie, who sat down.

"Hi, Allyson. I want to apologize for cutting your date with my brother short last night."

"It's okay." She smiled at the young woman, happy she had a brother to go to. "Was Zeke able to help you?"

Josie's brown gaze lit up. "He's working on it. I'm having trouble in one of my classes."

"I'm glad he can help you

"Me too." Josie leaned closer. "How involved with my brother are you?" She kept her voice low.

Allyson started to cough. Josie was direct, that was for sure. "That's between your brother and me."

"Please. My brother rarely dates, and he never has a woman over to his home."

"Josephine."

Both looked up to see Zeke standing there with his arms crossed over his chest, looking sexy and a bit perturbed.

"Ummmm…hi, brother." Josie winked at Allyson. "And don't call me by *that* name." She pushed back her chair and stood. "Enjoy lunch." With a wave, she was off.

"I don't ever remember being that carefree," Allyson said as Zeke took the seat Josie had vacated.

"To be young and not have a care in the world," Zeke said. There were lines of fatigue around his eyes. "I hope she wasn't annoying you."

"She wasn't. I think she's trying to figure out what's going on between us." Not that Allyson blamed Josie. She had a feeling that's what siblings did.

"Yeah, well, I should warn you that she told our parents about you."

"Is that a problem?" She stiffened.

Zeke's eyes narrowed. "Not for me, but they'd like to meet you. Is that an issue?"

"Oh?" She hadn't thought of that. "Can we put them off for a while?" She didn't fully answer his question.

"I'll try. Do you not want to meet them?"

Of course, he'd call her out on it. "It's not that." She twisted her hands together in her lap. "Zeke, I told you a little bit about my parents."

"Yes."

"Well, they weren't good role models, so I'm not sure I'm the right person to take home to your parents."

"Oh, sweetheart." He stretched his hands across

the table and waited until she put her hands in his. "I think they'd love you and you them, but if it's too early, that's all right. Everything in its time, right? I'll explain to them, and they'll wait until you're ready." He squeezed her hands.

If I ever am. She didn't say the words to Zeke. She didn't want to upset him. "Have you eaten yet?"

"No, I was waiting for you." When he called earlier and asked her to meet him here, she was surprised but glad.

"What will you have?"

"Today's special and a diet soda."

"You got it." Zeke's smile brightened Allyson's heart. "Be right back."

Allyson watched Zeke. Damn, the man had a fine ass. Firm. And his jeans gripped it just right. Heat flared in her belly. Her cell phone pinged, and she opened her bag where she'd placed the red folder with the questionnaire.

Oh hell, it was her boss. "Hey, Wes."

"Allyson. We might have an issue."

"Let me guess, Starr Construction called you." Zeke came back and placed the number at the end of the table.

She covered her phone. "My boss. It should only take a minute."

He nodded and rose, but she waved him back into his chair.

"Yes. They're not happy."

"I bet they're not. Check your inbox. I sent you the detailed report. Wes, there are violations all over the place, including inferior construction."

"Hold on a sec." She could hear the clicking of keys. "Holy crap."

"Yeah, I was livid. I don't know what Rudy has been doing with them, but what I saw today was unacceptable."

"Yep. Okay, no worries. I'll get on this. Sorry to bug you."

"You're just doing your job." She hung up.

"Problems at work?" Zeke asked.

"It's fine." She shook her head. "Which reminds me. The new home construction you're doing out on Pioneer, would ten Monday morning work?" She'd gotten notification of the permit being granted as she left the office today.

Zeke pulled out his phone. "That's perfect."

Allyson noted it in her calendar and put her phone away.

"Are we still on for tonight?" he asked.

"Yes." She was driving out to Zeke's again tonight, and they were going to finish up with the questionnaire and talk about their relationship. The idea sent shafts of excitement through her veins. Maybe there was a little bit of apprehension there, too, but mainly excitement. She wanted to try this with Zeke.

"Now doesn't this look cozy," a male voice commented.

Allyson took a deep breath as she looked up. "Hello, Rudy." What the hell was he doing here?

"Rudy." Zeke's voice was hard.

Allyson shifted in her seat, and Zeke's gaze shifted to her before going back to Rudy.

"We're having a late lunch. Would you like to join us?"

Allyson's gaze went from Rudy to Zeke. He had to be kidding, inviting Rudy to join them.

"No, thank you. I'm grabbing something to go." Rudy's gaze hardened. "Starr Construction isn't happy with you, Allyson."

"That's their problem. Wes is aware of my report." She wasn't going to let Rudy bully her.

"We'll see." With that, he walked way.

"Why did you invite him to sit with us?" Allyson asked with a shudder.

"I might not like the man, but this way, he can't say anything negative about us having lunch together."

"Oh, I didn't think about it like that." Not that it mattered. Rudy would find a way to twist it and spread rumors, no matter what Zeke did. Her boss was aware that she was seeing Zeke. He did warn her if Rudy started making too big a fuss and others thought it was an issue, she might have to let Rudy take over all of Zeke's jobs, and she would work with Starr.

Megan walked up with their food and drinks, placed them on the table, and then bustled away. "Thank goodness, I'm hungry." Allyson picked up her Panini and took a big bite.

"Did you miss breakfast?"

"Power bar on the run." Thanks to Starr

Construction. Their guy had been a half-hour late meeting her, and then she'd had to write up the lengthy report. And, of course, there was Rudy.

"We need to talk about your eating habits."

Her eyebrows rose. "What?"

"Yes, but not now. Eat up because you need the protein and carbs."

"Are you saying I'm too skinny?" That was a first.

"No. You are perfect." He grinned and leaned forward. "Perfect enough to take a bite out of."

Heat filled her face. "Zeke." Her voice was soft.

"Eat, sweetheart. Tonight, we finish up our talk and make a plan."

"Looking forward to it." She gave him what she hoped was a sassy grin before going back to her food.

Chapter 7

"Your questionnaire is all filled out," Zeke said later that night, after they had a dinner of Asian food at his house.

"I finished it up. And before you ask, Dani helped me when I had some questions."

"Good." He flipped through the pages a second time. "We're compatible with kink, but I do have some questions for you."

"Okay."

Her eyes were bright, and Zeke hoped he wouldn't scare her away. What was he thinking? If she was going to run, she would have done it before now. "On suspension, you put a soft limit, but on whole body suspension bondage you checked it as a hard limit."

"I did." She tilted her head. "Was that wrong?"

"No." He placed the questionnaire on the side table and faced her as they sat on his sofa. "I'm mildly into suspension. Have you ever heard of Shibari?" She shook her head. "Shibari is a type of bondage. A very intricate bondage done with ropes."

"Okay." She shifted.

"Once a person is bound, then they can be

suspended either from rings or other apparatuses."

Her eyes grew wide. "And you want to do that with me?"

"Eventually, if you wanted. I'm not a suspension master or anything. I've had a few subs who liked it, but if I don't do it again, I won't miss it. If you decide you want to try, we can, but it will take a long time to build you up to that point. Shibari can be intricate and sensual if you do it right."

"Can you explain more?"

She shifted closer to him. Good. Allyson was intrigued. "Let me show you." He stood. "Be right back." He went into his bedroom, then into his walk-in closet where he kept his bookcase full of kink books.

He pulled out two. They would be the best ones to show her how rope bondage worked, including suspension. When Zeke sat down, his thigh rubbed hers. "These are the best two books."

"May I see?" She held her hand out for them.

Zeke put the first one in her hand. She flipped through the pages, occasionally stopping to study the picture and reading before continuing. "It's almost like a step-by-step how-to manual."

"Yes. These two books were put out by a couple of guys who saw the need for instruction books. I love their work. I spent some time learning from them in San Francisco years ago."

"Why Shibari?" She handed him the first book but didn't ask to see the second one.

"It helps me focus."

"Who taught you?"

"It was my mentor in the lifestyle. He sat me down when he saw me losing focus on what I was doing in a scene. He grabbed some string and taught me several ties." Dom Alexander was in his mid-forties when Zeke met him, and he'd seen a lot. Zeke had soaked up all the knowledge he could.

"Showing you how to tie knots settled you down?" She tilted her head in the way only she could. "I don't get it."

"I didn't either at first." Zeke reached over and plucked a ball of string out of the drawer in table next to the sofa. "Ordinary string." He unwound a piece and then broke it off. "Now, ideally, this would be rope, but you're not ready for that yet." He took her right hand in his. "See, what he did was to get me to focus in on what I was doing."

Zeke wound the string around her wrist, then began to wrap it around her hand and between her fingers, careful not to pull too tight. "By handing me rope and instructing me, my need for control of the details came out. But it also made me focus on what I was doing." He kept talking as he encased her hand in string.

He could do that now. In the beginning, he'd been totally silent as he tied up a willing sub. "I started off with string, then moved to scarves for bondage purposes, and finally to rope, then Shibari."

"When did suspension come into play?" Her voice was soft, her breathing shallow.

"A couple of years ago, I watched a

demonstration on it and wanted to try." He carefully tied off the string and checked his work, making sure it wasn't too tight or cutting her circulation off. "Wiggle your fingers, please."

She did. Good. The movement was easy.

"After the Shibari demonstration, I talked with the Dom giving it. He offered to teach me. I took him up on it." He held her hand up. "What do you think?"

"Oh, wow." She turned her hand over in his and then back again. "That's intricate, yet I can barely feel it."

"Rope would be heavier and done differently. With the string, I'm able to get between your fingers easier, but the concept is the same. Also, with rope, the knots can be placed strategically." He pulled off another piece of string. "So with suspension, I would do this." He threaded the new piece through the design on the back of her hand, then held the ends together, and raised his hand. Hers followed.

"Goodness." Her breathing increased, and her skin flushed. This was exciting to her. Good. He was making progress.

"Now, with Shibari, I'd have tied the rope all over your body, placing the knots in strategic positions where they would arouse you but also have you within my control."

"That sounds wonderful."

Zeke took his gaze away from her hand at her breathless words. Her eyes were bright. Yes, she was finding this intensely seductive and sensual.

"We'll get there." He lowered her hand to his lap

and began to undo the design.

"I almost don't want you to remove it."

He grinned. "We can experiment more, but not tonight." Zeke set the string aside but kept her hand in his. "Okay with whole body now?"

"Soft limit, but it's one I'll want to discuss before we do."

"Agreed. Now, schedules."

"Schedules?"

"Yes, time for us to see each other."

"Oh. Well, for obvious reasons, weekends are best."

"I agree, but there's a slight problem there." Zeke had talked with Max about letting Allyson know about his work at the club. Max told him it was fine.

"What kind of problem?"

"I work at Wicked Sanctuary Friday and Saturday nights." Her mouth formed an O, but she didn't say a word. "Have I shocked you?"

"Yes…no. I didn't realize you worked there."

"It's a relatively new thing. Max needed some DM help and asked if I wanted to work for him on weekends."

"DM?"

"Dungeon monitors. You must have had them at the parties you went to."

"There was like a bouncer guy, but he was mainly by the door."

Zeke frowned. "There should always be a monitor nearby when playing."

"What do you do?"

"I basically supervise the play space. When couples play at the club, we monitor them to make sure nothing goes wrong. For example, if a sub calls out their safe word, we make sure the Dom stops."

"That makes sense."

"We also make sure no one causes any trouble."

"Do you get a lot of troublemakers?" A frown marred her forehead.

"Not really. We've had a few incidents but nothing that couldn't be handled."

"So what time does that leave us? We both work weekdays."

"We have some options. Dinner most nights of the week, making sure we're done by ten." He rubbed her knuckles. "There is also Wicked Sanctuary. If you joined, I have downtime before and after my shift, depending on what hours I'm working." Her eyes widened, but she stayed silent. "If you're more comfortable being private for right now, I have Saturdays free until about six, and I have Sunday afternoons."

"Can we try Saturdays first. I'm open to joining Wicked Sanctuary, but I'd like to get my feet wet before I jump in."

"That works. Questions?"

"A million." She flashed him a grin. "How do we do this?"

"We set a time for you to arrive Saturday, then we'll sit down and discuss what we're going to do that day."

"Negotiations."

"Yes. Once we get more familiar with each other, we won't need to do it as much."

"Okay." She leaned forward. "Please, kiss me."

He was surprised by her request but lowered his mouth to hers. Within a minute, their tongues were dueling and tasting. Hands roamed over bodies. His cock stiffened.

The next thing he knew, Allyson's hands were on his bare chest. When had she unbuttoned his shirt?

God, her touch was light, but it burned all the way to his bones. He slid his palm to her chest and caressed her breast. Even with the fabric of her clothing in the way, her nipple became taut.

"I want to taste you," he whispered against her lips.

Her hands dropped from his chest, and Zeke was about to protest, when she whipped her shirt up and over her head. Her bra disappeared a second later.

He dipped his head and took her right nipple in his mouth. Allyson's soft moan made his dick jump. He laved one nipple before moving to the other.

"More, Zeke," she whispered.

He wanted nothing more than to strip her bare. He lightly bit her nipple before lifting his head. "Sweetheart." Her eyes were slumberous and her lips plump from their kiss. "It's getting late, and we both have work tomorrow."

She groaned. "Damn." Allyson straightened up in his hold. "Where the hell did my bra go?"

Zeke found the scrap of fabric hanging off the back of the sofa. He held it by the straps for her to put her arms into. Before he fastened it for her, he placed a kiss on the top of each breast.

"Saturday, I'm going to feast on those breasts." His voice was husky with desire.

"I can't wait." She pulled her shirt back on. "And I get to feast on you." She leaned over and placed a kiss on his chest.

"Deal." He stood and almost moaned. His cock was protesting being confined to his pants. Zeke walked Allyson to her car.

"Saturday at eleven," he said.

"I'll be here."

"Think about me." He leaned inside the open window and kissed her hard and fast. "Call me when you get home. Not negotiable."

"Yes, Sir."

The Sir went straight to his dick. Zeke forced himself to step back and watched Allyson until he could no longer see her taillights. This woman had him tied up in more knots than a Shibari master.

* * * *

Allyson pulled up to Zeke's house Saturday. Her hands shook as she closed the door to her truck. She took a deep breath. There was nothing to be nervous about. The front door opened, and Zeke stood there. What little breath she had whooshed out of her.

He was wearing a pair of loose fitting black pants, a half-open black shirt, and a shit-eating grin on his face. "Are you going to stand out there all day?"

"Maybe." Her stomach fluttered with a million butterflies, but she walked to him.

Zeke took her hands in his. "I can see your nervousness. Why?" He tugged her into the house.

"I'm not sure." Allyson kicked off her sandals and allowed Zeke to guide her into the family room.

"You have all the control here." He released her hands.

A snort of laughter burst from her. "Don't you have that wrong?"

"No." He gestured for her to sit down and sat next to her. "I'm serious here. Nothing will happen that you don't want to happen." Zeke ran a finger over her cheek, and her nerves tingled with anticipation. "Safe word time. Choose a word you wouldn't use in everyday life."

Allyson thought for a moment. "Screwdriver."

Zeke tilted his head back and let out a belly laugh. "Good one. You get nervous, scared, anything doesn't feel right, say screwdriver, and I'll stop."

"What happens after you stop?"

"Then we discuss why you called your safe word. If we can talk it out and you're willing to continue, we will. If we talk it out and you're still uncomfortable, we move on."

"Move on? Like, walk away from each other?"

"No, sweetheart." His fingers curved around her neck. "We move on to something else."

"You scared me a bit there." Allyson relaxed into his touch on the back of her neck.

"Not my intention." He shifted. "Close your eyes."

She followed his instructions.

"That's it." His fingers caressed her skin. "Relax. Nothing is going to happen that you don't want." His voice was soft, almost hypnotic. "Today is all about learning about each other. No, don't tense up. Learning each other's bodies and what you like and don't like."

Allyson forced her muscles to loosen. She needed to quit taking him so literally or at least ask before she jumped to conclusions. "So I get to touch you?"

"Yes. Now there are a few ways we can do this. Go into my bedroom and lay on the bed, or stay here in the family room, either on the sofa or on the floor." His voice was closer now. "If you're comfortable, we could go out on the back patio on the oversized loungers and play there."

A small tremor went through her body. The bedroom seemed too intimate. The family room had merit, but it would be uncomfortable on the floor. Outside? "Can we try outside?"

"Of course." His breath brushed her cheek. "Open your eyes." She did and saw his deep brown gaze watching her. "Why don't you go out onto the patio, and I'll grab us some water. It's warm today, but not hot. But we still need to stay hydrated."

"Okay." Her voice was soft as he released her neck and stood. Allyson licked her lips and made her way out to the patio.

The oversized lounger had been moved closer to the house. Allyson looked around and her lips turned up. The way Zeke's porch was set up, and the fact he didn't have close neighbors, would protect them from prying eyes, if there were any. One would practically have to be right next to the patio to see them.

"Are you still nervous?" Zeke asked as he walked out, carrying several water bottles, and setting them on the side table.

"A little."

"Let's see what I can do to ease your nerves." He walked over to the lounger and patted the seat. Allyson sat down. "Now lean back and close your eyes."

She did as he asked, keeping her hands at her sides.

"Communication is important, so talk to me."

"All right." Allyson swallowed.

Zeke's fingers caressed her cheeks in a light touch, and her muscles uncoiled as her body relaxed onto the lounger.

"That's it. Relax."

His fingers skimmed over her neck to her throat. Every place he touched, her nerves came alive.

"You skin is pink, are you blushing or hot?"

"I'm hot from your touch."

"Good." He toyed with the buttons of her shirt. "May I unbutton your shirt?"

"Please."

Cool air caressed her skin a minute before his lips started kissing the tops of her breasts as his fingers caressed her abdomen. Allyson sucked in a breath.

"Too much?" he asked. His hot breath brushed over her sensitive skin.

"No." She squirmed on the lounger. "More."

"I see. Can you sit up?"

Allyson nodded.

Zeke put his arm around her back as she sat up. "I'm going to take your shirt off and remove your bra."

"Works for me." Actually, she wanted more. Neurons were firing like crazy in her brain, making her hot.

Zeke swiftly removed her top and bra. Her nipples tightened as the air caressed them. He applied slight pressure to her shoulders, and she laid back. Vulnerability hit her along with a good dose of lust.

"Beautiful breasts," Zeke whispered against her skin. "Ripe, pink nipples waiting for my touch."

Allyson's breathing increased, along with her anticipation. She didn't have to wait long. Zeke enclosed her right nipple with his lips. She arched her back, pushing it farther into his mouth, and she raised her hands to his head.

"I have to touch you."

"Of course." Zeke shifted. "Shirt is gone. Touch all you want."

While Zeke licked and bit her nipples, Allyson explored Zeke's back. His muscles played against her fingers, and she ran her hands up and down, her nails tracing his spine.

Heat filled her. Zeke's touch was different. She wasn't sure how she could explain it. She'd been with men before, but he was the opposite of them. They were more wham-bam-thank-you-ma'am guys, where Zeke wanted to take his time with her.

When his fingers skimmed the elastic of her shorts, she took a shuddering breath.

"What is it?" Zeke asked.

Allyson opened her eyes and stared down at him. "How can you read me so well?" She noticed that about him. He sometimes knew how she was feeling before she did.

"It's taught in Dom school."

"They have a Dom school?" Her lips twitched.

"Sort of." Zeke rested his head on her chest. "Doms have to learn to be Doms. So we are usually mentored by others. One of the things we're mentored on is watching how a sub reacts." He turned his head and blew air on her nipple. Her muscles contracted and then released with pleasure. "See? You find that pleasurable."

"I see." This was interesting. A crazy conversation to have in the middle of foreplay, but she did ask.

"Will it bother you if I remove your shorts?"

"No. That breath was one of anticipation, not fear."

"Good." Zeke sat up. "Lift your ass up, please." When she did, he swiftly pulled her shorts and underwear off.

"I thought you were just going to do my shorts?" She was exposed to him. Very exposed, yet she wasn't afraid. She was almost like a peacock that wanted to preen to show off.

"I couldn't resist." He placed a kiss on her belly and moved lower.

Her legs parted as he kissed the top of her mound.

Her pussy fluttered with want.

Zeke pushed her legs apart as he maneuvered between them.

Allyson squirmed. He was seeing all of her now. A quiver of passion shot through her veins.

"Pretty pink pussy." His breath brushed her thigh. Then he leaned down and licked.

She squeaked and shifted back against the cushions. Immediately, Zeke lifted his head.

"What is it? Did you not like it?" His voice held concern.

"It was a surprise." Now she was feeling foolish.

"Oh?" He walked his fingers up her thigh and toyed with her folds. "Have the men in your life not given you the ultimate oral pleasure?"

"Ummmm… No."

Zeke stared at her. "They were idiots. You marked this as a soft limit; are you okay to go on?"

"Yes, please. I was surprised." And a little more than turned on. She wanted to see and feel what he would do.

"I shall pleasure you, my lady." He winked at her before he lowered his head. This time, his fingers spread her apart, and then he licked.

The moan that left her lips was pure pleasure. Zeke was careful. He licked and sucked, but not to the point to throw her over into an orgasm. He kept her on the edge, and she was loving every minute of it.

Each nip, each lick sent her higher and higher. Her belly tightened, and tingles began shooting through her nerves.

"Come for me," he said, pausing.

"I…" She could barely catch her breath.

"You're right there." Zeke slipped two fingers into her pussy as his lips closed over her clit.

She cried out as the dam burst, and she fell over the edge. Her body shook. She tangled her fingers in his hair, holding him to her as she rode the wave of her orgasm.

"Oh dear God." Allyson released his head, and he leaned his cheek against her thigh as her body trembled in the aftermath. "I didn't mean to cut off your breathing."

"I'm fine, sweetheart." His voice was husky.

"I'm not sure I am." The waves of pleasure were still flowing over her. In all her play, she had never experienced feelings of this intensity.

Zeke's deep laugh reached her ears. "You will be. I'm not through with you yet."

"I hope not." Her breathing was finally settling down. She looked down at him. "Will you undress for me?" Her mouth watered in anticipation of seeing him.

"If you like."

"Please."

Zeke stood up and slipped his pants and underwear off. His cock was stiff. Her eyes widened.

"I didn't expect…"

"That I'd be hard for you?" He sat down, his hip brushing hers. "Honey, I'm always hard for you."

Heat flared deep within her, and she glanced down to see a blush rising over her breasts. "I didn't realize."

"Hey." He cupped her chin and turned her face to him. "I want you. That's a fact."

Her fingers curled around his dick, and he moaned. "Shall I do something to relieve you first?"

His eyes flared with passion. "As much as I'd like that, it wouldn't make things better."

"Why not?"

"Because my dick would be hard again after you finished. Maybe after we make love a few hundred times, it might give me a break."

Allyson's lips tilted up. "Then let's get started."

Zeke laughed. "Are you saying no more foreplay?"

"I'm saying I want you in me." More than anything she wanted to feel him deep within her.

"I can do that. Let me go get a condom." He started to rise. "I can't believe I forgot them."

"It's okay." Allyson sat up and put her arms around his waist. "You've seen my medical report. All of the tests were clear, and I'm on the pill."

"And you've seen mine." He leaned over and brushed a kiss over her lips.

He tasted salty, and that's when she realized she was tasting herself on his lips. She bit her lower lip. This was so different from...everything.

"Come to me, my big, handsome Dom."

"As you wish, my delightful sub." Zeke lowered his body to hers, his cock brushing her entrance before demanding entry.

Inch by inch, Zeke pressed into her pussy and

retreated.

She shivered with each inch he slipped into her. He was big, hard, and all hers. His lips covered hers.

Allyson wasn't sure how long she could hold on. Her toes were already curling in need of release. But she wanted this to be good for Zeke.

"Get out of your head," Zeke mumbled against her lips. "I'm doing something wrong if you're thinking so much."

"You're doing everything right." She wouldn't let him think he wasn't.

Her hips shifted as he pumped in and out of her. She turned her head away from his kisses, trying to catch her breath.

"You feel so good," he whispered. "I've wanted to do this for a while now."

"I'm glad you persisted." She moaned as he shifted his hips. "I…" She couldn't complete her thought as another climax roared through her.

Zeke thrust two more times before he shouted, and his release started. Their bodies writhed against each other until Zeke collapsed.

"Shit." He immediately rose off her body, his cock dragging against every nerve in her pussy. "Are you okay?"

"Well, since I can hear you, I can't be dead." She opened her eyes — hell, when had she closed them — to see him grinning down at her.

"I hope you're not dead." Laughter tinged his voice as he lay down next to her on the lounger, gathering her into his arms. "Rest."

Allyson rested her head on his chest, enjoying the feeling of his chest hair against her cheek and the beating of his heart against her ear. Maybe there was something to be said about being with the right man.

* * * *

A little over two weeks later, Allyson sat down in her office with a grin. Her relationship with Zeke was progressing, and they were learning about each other. They'd spent most of Sunday curled up on his sofa watching them.

He wasn't happy she wouldn't go to breakfast with his parents, but she told him it was too soon. It was. At least for her.

Allyson pushed her emotional baggage to the back of her head as her boss walked into her office.

"Hey, Wes. What's up?"

"Morning, Allyson." He stepped inside and pushed the door partially closed. Allyson sat up in her chair.

"What's wrong?"

"Rudy is making one hell of a fuss this morning, and he's gone to higher management, saying the work isn't being distributed in a fair manner. They want me to have you two switch off some jobs."

"But I've done nothing wrong." That meant she'd see less of Zeke. Her tummy tightened. Damn Rudy. He was friends with the guys from Starr Construction. Hell, he went out for beers with them, but because she was female, it was different? It shouldn't be, but it was.

"I know that. My boss does too, but he's getting

pressure from his boss, and for the moment, they're thinking this is the solution."

Allyson shook her head and pulled her files. She had five for Riggs and two for Starr. "How are we going to do this?"

"Give me job 1836, 1978, and 4432 from Riggs." She pulled the files and handed them to him. "I left you the other two jobs for specific reasons. I'm checking with Rudy later to get jobs for you."

"All right." She wondered why he left her those two jobs. She'd barely looked at them. Actually, the permit and the plans on one of them came through Friday as she was leaving.

"I'm sorry about this, Allyson. I have no choice here." Wes stood. "I know your work is above board."

"Thanks, Wes. It's not your fault." She watched him leave her office, then her phone rang. "This is Allyson."

"Good morning," Zeke's rich tone soothed her nerves.

"Good morning. What can I do for you?" She wondered why he was calling.

"I was wondering if you could meet me on one of the jobs this morning?"

She pulled up her calendar. Her morning was open. "Sure. Which job?" She hoped it wasn't one she just gave to Wes for Rudy.

"2982, technically, still within the county's jurisdiction."

Allyson opened the file. "Right on the edge in the unincorporated area."

"Yep. Can you meet me there at eleven?"

"Sure. I got the permit and the plans on Friday."

"Yes. Pull into the parking lot when you get here, and I'll come out with the owner. There's some paperwork we have to discuss before we start."

She looked at the file. "You're being mysterious."

"You'll understand why. See you in a couple of hours." The line went dead.

Allyson spread the small version of the plans on her desk but couldn't see anything different about this job. It looked like a remodel on an existing building. She read the permit over, and yep, it was clearly a remodel of business space. Okay. She'd put the address into her phone GPS because it was off the beaten track, and she didn't want to get lost.

* * * *

At five after eleven, Allyson pulled over to the side of the road. She was lost. Her GPS couldn't even figure out where this place was. It had only taken her so far, and she thought she could figure it out. Nope. She dialed Zeke's number.

"Allyson, are you okay?"

"I'm fine. But I'm lost."

"I should have picked you up or at least met you and had you follow me. Where are you?"

She told him where she was on the main road and the mile marker post. "Okay, can you put your phone on speaker, you're nearly here."

"On speaker." Allyson placed her phone in the holder.

"Go straight, once you hit mile marker fifteen, go

about a quarter of a mile, and on the left you'll see a driveway. Turn into the driveway and follow it. It will bring you to the parking lot."

"All right." Allyson spied the road marker and noted the mileage, then kept her eyes peeled. Yep, there it was. She missed it driving back and forth. "I'm good now. See you in a minute."

Allyson pulled into the parking lot and a big… She wanted to call it a house, but it didn't have any windows. Zeke and another man stood next to Zeke's truck. She parked next to Zeke.

He was at her door before she could open it. "I forgot how hard this place is to find if you don't know where it is," he said.

"It's okay. Not the first time I've gotten lost on these back roads." She grabbed her clipboard and shut the door to her truck.

"Max, this is Allyson Young with the city inspector's office. Allyson, Max Preston, owner of Wicked Sanctuary."

Allyson stopped in her tracks. This was Wicked Sanctuary?

"I think you shocked her."

"Mr. Preston, it's nice to meet you." Allyson held out her hand.

"It's Max, and it's great to finally meet you." He shook her hand. "Zeke has told me a lot about you."

"Oh?" Allyson glanced over at Zeke, who was smiling.

"Only good stuff," Zeke said.

"What paperwork did you need me to fill out?"

Allyson asked.

"I like her. Gets right to the point." Max motioned to the back of Zeke's truck where the tailgate was down with a makeshift table top on it. "It's an NDA about the club."

"NDA?"

"Standard with the club," Zeke said, handing her the papers.

Allyson read them through. Nothing she hadn't seen before. She could understand Max's need for that. Thank goodness this hadn't been one of the jobs she had to hand over to Wes for Rudy.

She signed the bottom of the NDA and handed it to Zeke, who handed it to Max. "Before I forget, Zeke, Rudy is making waves, so you're going to be dealing with him on some of your other jobs."

"They took you off my jobs?" Zeke stiffened.

"Three of them, but not this one. Thank goodness."

"Ah, that's what Wes meant when I called him," Max said.

"You know my boss?" Allyson stared at Max.

"Yes. Zeke assured me you wouldn't have any issues working at the club, but your co-worker might. I need someone I can trust, so I made a call."

"No worries."

"Shall we get this moving?" Max asked.

"Ohhh, someone sounds testy. Did you not get your caffeine this morning?" A woman with black hair walked over to them.

"Sierra." Max stared at the woman, and Allyson

burst out laughing at the face Sierra made. Max turned his gaze to her.

"I'm sorry; the look you gave her was, shall we say, intense, and her reaction was not what I expected." Allyson shrugged.

"Sierra, Max's fiancée. Let me go grab him a mug of coffee, and we can start." Sierra disappeared inside and returned with a large travel mug. She handed it to Max.

"Thank you, love." He took a long drink, then gave her a kiss. "All right, expansion of the club." Max led them around the building to the north wall. "Based on the plans Gabriel drew up, we're going to remove this wall." He patted the building. "And we're going to expand out."

"I looked at the small plans I have on file." Allyson glanced at the foliage and trees. Since this was private property, there wasn't a requirement to replace the green space, and she didn't see any reason to. There were plenty of trees and foliage even with the expansion. "Max, how much of this land do you own?" She hadn't pulled the full property records.

"Roughly fifty acres. Our private home is on one acre, the club is slightly below two acres."

"When the club is done it will be closer to three acres," Zeke said.

"If you're worried about the trees, we're going to replace them further out," Max said. "There are some bald spots that were discovered a few weeks ago when a survey was done. I'll have new trees planted out there."

"Since this is private property, that's up to you." Allyson walked around, taking note of the soil and how far out the building would extend. She glanced at the plans in her hand. "Looks like you're expanding the bathrooms and other areas?"

"Yes." Zeke pointed the changes out on the plans. "Since the club is getting busier, I suggested we expand the bathrooms and the entryway."

"Makes sense. How long do you think this is going to take?" This was a large job.

"Once you give the okay, we'll start clearing, level the land, make sure the utilities are good, and start on the foundation. That should take about a month or so. The building will take several," Zeke said.

"Summer is the best time to do it," Max said. "We have light later, and since the club doesn't open until seven, the construction crews will be long gone before that."

"Makes sense. I don't see any issues at this point. I'll need to follow up at each stage." Allyson jotted down some notes. "Are you going to expand the parking lot as well?" she asked as they walked to the front.

"Yes." Max rubbed the back of his neck.

"It's here on the plans." Zeke ran his finger over the drawing. "There's no trees in the area, just foliage. But once we expand it, we're going have trees planted and more foliage to spruce up the area."

"I've been told it's a little sparse." Max glanced over at Sierra, who grinned.

"What about lighting?" She noticed the lighting

on the building itself.

"We're going to make use of the building and put up flood lights to illuminate the parking lot better. If needed, we'll put some subtle lighting on the edges so there are no dark corners, but not enough to affect local wildlife," Zeke said.

"You've thought of everything."

"I hope so." Zeke's hand brushed the back of hers.

"That's all I need to see for today," Allyson said.

"Not the inside?" Max asked.

"Not today. Eventually, but since it's taking a wall out, Zeke knows what to do."

Max nodded. "Thank you for coming out."

"Part of the job."

"It was nice to meet you," Sierra said. "Make sure to bring her out one night, Zeke."

"And with that, we'll bid you good-bye." Max took Sierra by the arm and led her inside.

"What did she mean?" Allyson asked Zeke.

"Let's walk to your truck." Zeke cupped her elbow. "Sierra is hoping you'll come to the club with me one night."

"Oh?" While they'd talked about it in the beginning, he hadn't mentioned it again.

"No pressure. Which jobs did you lose?"

"Rudy got the new medical clinic over on fifth, the new library, and the home remodel. Then we'll end up splitting any new jobs, unless the higher ups decide differently."

"That's it for a while. My crews are tapped out, especially with taking on the club expansion."

"I'm happy you're so busy."

"I am too." He leaned down. "Dinner tonight?"

"Can't. Remember, I promised Dani we'd have a girls' night." She'd been spending her evenings with Zeke and missed seeing her friend.

"Right."

Her phone beeped. "Damn, I need to go. I'm supposed to meet with the Starr Construction guys."

"Be careful." He held open the truck door for her.

"I will be." Allyson climbed in.

Zeke shut the door. "Call me if you need anything or get lost."

Allyson shook her head.

* * * *

Zeke stepped out of the way and watched her back out and drive off. He hated the idea she was getting more Starr jobs. Something odd was going on there.

Zeke rubbed his forehead as he walked back inside the club. Max wanted to talk after Allyson left. He found Max in his office. "What did you need?"

"I wanted to know if you'd be available to cover the club all shift Friday and Saturday this weekend?" Max asked.

"Let me look." Zeke pulled up his calendar. "I don't see any reason why not."

"Good. You and Colby will be in charge, with Noah and Oliver as backups."

"What's happening, Max?" It wasn't like Max to take a weekend off. No matter how much everyone tried to lighten his load.

"I promised Sierra a weekend away. I want to make sure there's coverage."

"That makes sense."

"I like Allyson," Max said.

"She's fun." Zeke didn't know what else to say.

"If she wants to join, all she'll need to do is fill out the background check. I'll waive the classes since I know you've been teaching her."

"Yeah." It wasn't like he hadn't talked about Allyson. He had. "I'll bring it up to her again."

"All right. If you can stop by Thursday night, I'll have an extra set of keys for you then, and a couple of gate codes you can use for the construction crews coming in."

"You're setting up special codes?"

"Yes. I know all your guys are signing NDAs but the delivery drivers are not, and I want to make sure I know who is using the codes. Plus, they'll only be active during certain hours."

"Got it." Zeke left. Time to get back to his job. He was going to miss seeing Allyson tonight, but it would give him time to plan out Sunday's playtime.

Chapter 8

Zeke looked over his handywork early Sunday afternoon. He'd cut short breakfast with his family to get home and prepare for Allyson. He should be tired after pulling full shifts at the club on Friday and Saturday, but he wasn't.

Maybe because he was seeing Allyson. It was the only day they could play. They'd been talking about her joining him at the club, and she wanted to try. So he'd asked Max about giving her the background check to fill out.

They'd do that first thing. It was a beautiful day; too bad they couldn't play outside, but with what he wanted to do, it was better to be inside. Zeke had never played much outside the club, so this was new to him.

He'd rearranged the family room, put an air mattress on the floor, along with several mats. He had his toys and ropes set out on the table. They were covered so he wouldn't scare Allyson. Although she didn't seem the type to scare easily.

A knock on the door and he glanced at the clock. One, right on time. He opened the door to see Allyson. She had on a flowery sundress and sandals.

"Hi," she said.

He pulled her into his arms and kissed her. They were both breathless when he lifted his head.

"That was a nice greeting," she said.

"I hope so." He guided her into the house. She left her sandals by the front door, along with her purse.

"What's on tap for today?" she asked.

"First off, I have the background check for the club for you to fill out." They moved into the family room.

Allyson stopped and stared at the changes. "You certainly have something else planned."

"I do. Let's sit." He guided her to the kitchen table and pulled a chair out for her. On the table was a pen and the background check paperwork.

Allyson stared at it.

"Is there a problem?" Zeke wondered if she'd balk at the check. He'd told her about it, and she said she was fine, but now something was making her hesitate.

"How confidential is this?"

"Max sends the background check to a contact at the police department. He runs the check and sends the information to Max. Max told me he is the only one who reads it." Her shoulders sagged. She was concerned about it. "Is there something in your past that makes you worried?"

"Maybe some stuff from when I was a teenager." She shifted in her seat.

"Juvie records are sealed. And we all did things as teenagers most of us later regret."

"Did you?" She picked up the pen.

"Yes. Staying out too late and worrying my parents was one of them." He always regretted that he caused his parents pain when he didn't come home at curfew.

"At least they cared," she mumbled. Not the first time she'd said something like that, but he knew if he tried to pry more information out of her, she'd clam up. "Done." She put the pen down.

"Thank you. I'll give this to Max tomorrow."

"How long before we know I passed?"

"At least a week." He drew her to her feet. "For today, I want to do a little bit of bondage play."

"All right."

Zeke pulled her into the family room. "That's the reason for the air mattress and mats. Actually, the air mattress is for you, mats for me."

Allyson nodded. "Shall I undress?"

"Yes. And Dom/sub protocols are in order."

"Yes, Sir."

Zeke grinned. They'd been working on that when they were in play mode. Allyson confided in him that, when she played before, she refused to call the Doms Sir or Master. He suspected it was because she didn't trust or respect them. Something they didn't have to worry about.

Each day, her trust in him grew. As for respect, she'd had that since they started working together.

When Allyson was nude, he helped her lie down on the air mattress.

"I'm going to do some simple Shibari ties on your

ankles and wrists."

"Okay, Sir."

Zeke picked up the hemp rope he'd laid out. "What I'm going to do is called a single column Shibari tie." He positioned her arm out to her side and then wrapped the rope above the joint, making sure he could get his fingers underneath. He wrapped it several times, twisting the rope and taking the loop end under the wrap to create a knot. It was a simple tie, and within five minutes, he had her wrists and ankles in the ties.

Next, he grabbed four single strands of rope and threaded them through the loop at the end of the ties on her wrists and ankles. This was another reason for the rearrangement of the furniture. He needed places to tie the rope off.

He used the sofa legs for her right arm and leg. For the left, he used two of the overstuffed chairs. When he finished the ties, he stepped back and looked at her.

Her skin was flushed and her breathing shallow. She was aroused by this. That's what he wanted. "If anything starts to go to sleep or feel numb, tell me right away."

"Yes, Sir."

"We've talked about using toys." He picked up a vibrator from the table, along with nipple clamps and a bullet.

"We have, Sir."

Her breathing sped up, and Zeke hid a grin. There were so many things he could do to her with her tied up. "I think first I need to warm you up."

"If I get any hotter, Sir, I'm going to burst into flames."

Zeke belly laughed. "That's my girl." He lowered his body onto the mats around the air mattress. "I think"—he placed a kiss on her right nipple—"someone is eager." Another kiss on her left nipple. Goosebumps broke out on her skin. "Are you cold?"

"No, Sir."

"I hope not." He laved her nipples, making sure the peaks were super hard before he picked up the nipple clamps. "I'm going to put nipple clamps on you."

A small whimper came from her lips. Zeke glanced up at her. There was a little bit of apprehension in her eyes.

"They're called tweezer clamps." He held one up. "See, rubber tips to protect you and a little ring I push up to create compression. I'll be gentle."

"Please, Sir."

Zeke placed the first one on her nipple and adjusted the compression. When Allyson hissed, he stopped. "Okay?"

"Yes, Sir." Her breathing was choppy.

He quickly did the second one. "You know, you look good adorned in nipple clamps. Maybe we'll work up to ones that dangle with little jewels I can play with as I fuck you."

Another whimper escaped her lips, and Zeke hid a smile. His lady was turned on. Good. That's where he wanted her. He placed a soft kiss on each nipple before kissing his way to her pussy. Her hips wiggled a bit. He hadn't tied her so tight she couldn't move a little.

"Zeke, Sir," she called out when he flicked her clit with his tongue.

"So sensitive." His fingers closed around the vibrator. He turned it on low and teased her opening with it before slowly sliding it into her pussy.

"Sir," she moaned. "That feels different."

"Different how?" It was a standard vibrator. He hadn't gotten around to talking with Damon about any special toys, at least not yet.

"Not as warm as you are, Sir."

"I see." Zeke watched as he pulled the vibrator out and pushed it back in. He noted the feel of her muscles gripping the toy, the way her body flushed, and her tiny moans of pleasure. The Dom inside him preened at being able to affect her like that. The man was pleased as well.

He needed to watch how long he left the nipple clamps on since it was her first time using them. Zeke continued to stroke her with the vibrator, feeling her muscles clamping down against the toy.

"Talk to me, sweetheart."

"What should I say, Sir?" Her voice was soft and breathless. "My nipples don't hurt, yet they feel very sensitive."

"Keep going."

"My pussy wants more… Actually, it wants you more than the toy, Sir."

"Is that right?" Was she trying to top from the

bottom? He didn't think so; he asked for her opinion.

"Yes, Sir. The toy isn't you, Sir."

He didn't want their play to end too early, but his cock was already demanding release. Patience, he reminded himself.

"Not yet, sweetheart." He turned the vibrator up and reached for the bullet. While Allyson's clit was sensitive to his tongue, he wondered how it would do with the bullet.

Using his free hand, he nestled the bullet against her clit. He hadn't thought this through, rare of him. "I'm going to release your legs." He removed the bullet then quick-released her ankles. Now he could work with this. "Close your legs and keep the vibrator within you."

"Yes, Sir." Her voice was strained, and he realized she was on edge already. The vibrator wasn't on that strong, so it wouldn't throw her over. Not yet. He went back to the table and grabbed some more rope. "Bend your knees, feet flat on the mattress." She did and moaned at the change of position of the vibrator.

Zeke make quick work of binding her lower legs, before binding right above her knees. He left slack in that rope because he was going to need it. He tossed the extra rope aside.

"Relax your legs." He pressed his hand between her thighs, and her legs parted until the rope went taut. Good. Exactly how he wanted her.

"What did you do, Sir?" Her eyes widened when she opened them. "Oh dear God," she whispered.

"This was not planned, but since you're being

such a good sub…" This time, when he nestled the bullet on her clit, it stayed there. Oh yes, this was going to be interesting. Zeke checked her nipples. Those clamps needed to come off soon. Zeke reached between her legs increased the vibrator and then turned the bullet on.

"Damn, Sir," Allyson said.

"Just to keep you on edge. But we need to get those nipple clamps off." Shifting, Zeke brushed her hip. "The blood is going to go rushing back into your nipples when I take the clamps off. It can be painful, but pleasure should follow."

Her eyes widened. Zeke leaned over, slipped the clamp off her right nipple and then placed his mouth over her nipple.

"Ahhhh." Allyson arched her back as he laved her nipple. When she settled down, he lifted his head and did the same thing with the left nipple.

Her cry this time wasn't as deep, but she pressed herself up to him. He waited until she collapsed on the mattress.

"Are you okay?" Her eyes were closed, her mouth open as she panted for breath.

"My nipples are on fire, Sir." She tugged her arms.

"Tolerable?"

"Yes, Sir." She shifted her feet.

"I think maybe it's time to take care of another part of you." Zeke turned the vibrator on full, and the bullet up to the second speed.

"Oh fuck," she whispered, her head going from

side to side.

Zeke saw her toes curl into the mattress and the flush moving up her body. "Oh, Zeke, it's too much."

"Is it?" He pressed the button for the bullet to go to the third speed.

Allyson cried out, her back arching off the mattress as she pressed her heels down. Her body shook with the force of her climax. He leaned over and kissed her cheek. "So pretty when you come."

She rode out the first climax, but when he upped the speed on the bullet, she screamed. "Too much. Screwdriver!"

Zeke turned off the toys, released the ropes from her legs, and pulled them from her body. Then he untied her wrists. He gathered her into his arms. Her body shook with tremors. "Sweetheart, are you okay?"

"I…" She fought to get a breath. "Too much pleasure. It overwhelmed me."

"I'm not going to say that's a bad thing. Let's get more comfortable." Zeke positioned her on the mattress as he got to his knees, then he lifted her into his arms as he stood.

He carried her over to the sofa, where he sat down with her on his lap and pulled a blanket over her.

"Did I ruin our play?" she asked softly, her head against his shoulder, her eyes still closed.

"You didn't. You did exactly what you needed to do." He checked her wrists. There were no marks or bruises. He checked her legs—the same. She trembled.

"Are you sure you're okay?"

"Yes." Her fingers caressed his cheek. He gazed down at her. Her blue eyes were clear. "Small climax aftershocks."

He nodded. "Nothing hurts."

"Everything hurts in a delicious way." She grinned at him. "I've never climaxed that hard."

"Are you giving me a challenge?"

"No, Sir. Just stating a fact."

Zeke chuckled. "Rest for a bit."

"Yes, Sir." Her eyes closed, and she relaxed in his hold.

Zeke blew out a breath. It wasn't the first time he had a sub safeword on him, but hearing it from Allyson's lips was different. He'd have to be more careful next time. Because there would be a next time.

* * * *

A week later, between the home remodel and the new library, Zeke was about to pull his hair out by the roots. Rudy was being a pain in the ass. Zeke pulled up to the library to see his foreman and Rudy arguing.

"Zeke, thank goodness. Would you explain to him that we're not required to file for a new permit for every little change?" Larry drew his hand through his graying hair.

"I've got it, Larry." Zeke sent his foreman on the way and then looked at Rudy. "What is the issue now?" There had been nothing but issues with Rudy.

"The foundation isn't up to code," Rudy said, rocking on his feet.

"I can assure you it is." Zeke pulled up the

paperwork on his tablet. "Right here, it's passes every single test you demanded, and the information was passed to your office."

"But you didn't file that there was a new concrete company used."

Zeke fought to keep his temper under wraps. "Because I'm not required to. My regular guy was booked. I used another company so we could get this done on time. I made sure everything was up to code." And then some. He hated that his normal guy couldn't fit him in, but understood.

"This is going into my report. Also the green replacement isn't sufficient."

"Really?" Zeke knew it was. This guy liked throwing things in the way. "Why don't you write up what you think is missing, because I'm aware of how much green space we removed and how much we're adding."

"I'll do that. I won't allow you to cut corners like you did with Allyson." Rudy flipped through his paperwork. "By the way, the plans for the Wilkins' remodel have an issue. They're someone else's design."

"Excuse me?" Zeke's fingers curled into his palms.

"I said they're someone else's designs."

"They were done by the architect on record. Maybe you should talk to him."

"That's your job."

"Who is this accusation coming from?" Zeke wanted to tell Gabriel and see what was going on.

"Starr Construction," Rudy muttered.

"Figures."

"Here's the information. I'll watch for the new plans." Rudy handed him several pieces of paper and then walked away.

Zeke pulled out his cell phone. "Gabriel, we have a problem. Meet me at the office in twenty."

Anger churned in his gut. Starr construction. It figures. Zeke was beginning to wonder if Rudy was in their back pocket. First, he had to figure out what was going on. Jumping in his truck, he started the engine and drove to the office.

He didn't have a fancy office like Starr did. No, he rented a small office space in one of the downtown buildings that held an office for him and one for Gabriel. They had a community conference room they could use when needed. Instead of a receptionist, Zeke used a service if he or Gabriel didn't answer their phones.

Unlocking the door, Zeke went to his desk and started pulling up information on his computer. Gabriel walked in ten minutes later.

"What's the emergency?"

"Starr is claiming our plans on the Wilkins' remodel are stolen."

"The hell they are." Gabriel stormed out of Zeke's office and returned a minute later. "Here's the plans, the copyright information, and the filing letter signed and dated by the permit office."

Zeke glanced at the paperwork. Yep, this had all been done over six months ago. They hadn't started on the remodel until recently due to weather and not having enough staff.

"Sit down," Zeke said to Gabriel.

"What are you going to do?"

"Get to the bottom of this." Zeke picked up the phone and called the Code Enforcement Department. "Hi, Wes. Zeke Riggs here. I've got a problem I need your help with." Zeke outlined what was going on and agreed to meeting Wes at his office in an hour.

"Do you think that will help?" Gabriel asked.

"Yes. We have proof on your plans, plus a bunch of other stuff that Wes needs to know about."

"Good. I know this new inspector has been a thorn in our sides since he was assigned to us. Which reminds me, how is the Allyson doing?"

"She's good. We're progressing nicely." He'd talked with Gabriel about Allyson, not details, but he wanted to bounce ideas off Gabriel.

"Great. Is she going to join Wicked Sanctuary?"

"We're still talking about it." After she'd seen the club, she was curious. Zeke told her what he could. She was still thinking about it.

"Let's go to the Wes' office, I want to get this off our plates and get back to work," Gabriel said.

"Yeah, let's."

They spent two hours with Wes, not only showing him the plans and permit for the remodel, including the CAD drawings and copyright, but Zeke told him about the other jobs he was working with Rudy on and the issues.

Wes pulled several things up on his computer and

began printing things out. "I'll take care of this." He looked at Zeke. "You're in the clear. Keep moving forward with your projects."

"Thanks. I'm sorry to come to you with this, but it's gotten to the point I can't move forward unless something is done." Zeke didn't like going to someone's boss, but Rudy wouldn't work with him at all.

"I'm glad you did."

Gabriel and Zeke left Wes' office. "Want to go grab lunch?" Gabriel asked.

Zeke looked down the hall. Allyson's office door was closed, which meant she was out of the office or otherwise unavailable. "Sure, why not."

"I'm wounded. Second best." The grin on Gabriel's face made Zeke laugh.

"You're not as good looking as Allyson is."

Gabriel laughed.

* * * *

Allyson threw her bag down on the floor and flopped onto her office chair Friday mid-morning. Starr Construction was driving her crazy. Nothing they were doing was up to code. What the hell was Rudy doing when he worked with them?

She'd recently had an argument with the owner, not the first one, but it was the last one as far as she was concerned. This had gone on long enough. She'd already put in the paperwork for fining the company, but it was time to talk to Wes.

Gathering up all the files, she marched to Wes' office and knocked on the closed door.

"Come in."

Allyson opened the door. Wes sat behind his desk, which was covered in plans and papers.

"I can come back if you're busy."

"No, come on in. I have a feeling you're here about Starr?"

"Yes." She sat down on the chair in front of Wes' desk. "I issued paperwork to have them fined."

Wes sighed. "What did you find?"

"It's more what didn't I find." She handed the files over to Wes and watched as he flipped through them.

"What a mess," Wes muttered.

"It is. I don't know what Rudy was doing, but it wasn't work. They're using sub-standard materials, are out of code on most of their projects, and they refuse to correct the deficiencies. Today, I was patted on the head and told to be a good little woman and go back to my office. That men can handle the work."

"What?" Wes bellowed.

"I don't know what century the Starr owner is in, but I sort of let him have it." She wasn't proud she lost her temper, but she'd had enough.

Wes raised his eyebrows. "As long as we've worked together, Allyson, I've never seen you lose it."

"I did today. I'm sure he'll be calling to complain."

"Let him. I'll handle it. Are these all the Starr jobs you have?" He patted the files.

"Yes."

"All right. I'm transferring all the Riggs

Construction jobs back to you. You might need to talk with them to find out where everything sits until I can get the records from Rudy."

"So the bosses upstairs finally figured out what is going on?" That had only taken a month, but it was more than enough for her.

"No." He spread his hands out indicating everything on his desk. "And I can't talk about it at the moment. All I can say is several things have been brought to my attention, and I've done some checking."

"Okay." She stood. "I'll be in my office getting up to speed."

Allyson spent the next few hours going over what was in the files of the jobs she'd received back. There was a lot to catch up on.

Her cell rang. She answered it. "Hello."

"Hey, honey," Zeke's voice was cheerful.

"Hi." She sat back in her chair. "What's up?"

"Well, I was wondering, since it's Friday, if you wanted to do dinner and maybe come to Wicked Sanctuary with me?"

Allyson thought for a minute. "I'd love to." There was silence on the line. "Zeke?"

"I'm still here. I think you surprised me."

She laughed. "Glad I can still do that."

"We'll talk over dinner."

"Okay, but what kind of dress code for the club?" She knew they had one.

"No jeans or sneakers. Whatever you wore to the play parties should be fine."

Allyson thought. "Okay. Should I meet you somewhere?'

"Come to my house. I'll drive us."

"I meant for dinner." Zeke was always looking out for her.

"I did too. My place at five, then we'll go out, and then to the club."

"All right. See you later." She hung up with a smile on her lips. Tonight was the night she'd see the inside of Wicked Sanctuary.

A commotion in the hallway caught her attention. She went to the doorway of her office. Folks from HR and building security stood outside Wes' office.

"Please, everyone, stay back," one of the security officers said.

"What's going on?" one of the other people on the floor asked.

"I have no idea." What could be going on in Wes' office? She hoped he was okay. Just then, security escorted Rudy out of the office.

"I'll make you all regret this," Rudy yelled as he was led down the hall to the elevator.

Wes came out of his office and talked with Linda from HR, then they both looked at everyone lingering in the hall or outside their offices.

"Okay, everyone, conference room," Wes said.

Allyson shut her office door, followed the others into the conference room, and took a seat.

"I'm sure there will be rumors galore, but Rudy was fired for cause," Linda stated.

A murmur went through the room. Allyson sat in

her chair in shock. She'd talked with Wes a few hours ago.

"I know this is abrupt and a disturbance for all of you," Wes said. "I will be adding two new full-time staff in the coming weeks. That's it."

People shuffled out of the room. Wes caught Allyson by the arm before she could leave. "Stay for a minute."

Allyson's muscles froze. Oh shit, was she getting fired too? What had she done? Did Rudy accuse her of something? How would she fight this?

Linda and Wes waited until everyone left and shut the door.

"Sit, Allyson," Linda said. When Allyson didn't move, she continued. "You're not in trouble or anything like that."

Allyson released a pent-up breath and sat down. "Why?" She cleared her throat. "Why did you want me to stay?"

"Because I think you deserve an explanation of what happened," Wes said.

"And I agreed," Linda commented. "Rudy was let go because he was falsifying documents."

Allyson blinked several times, then it hit her. "The changes in the computer."

"That and more." Linda placed her hands on the table. "You alerted Wes to the issue; he alerted me and IT. It was all traced back to Rudy."

"The information you gave me this morning was kind of the cherry on top of the cake type of thing," Wes said. "I was already going over all of the work

Rudy had been doing. I've been getting complaints for weeks."

"Riggs Construction," Allyson whispered.

"Yes, plus some out of town sub-contractors. Rudy wasn't subtle about what he was doing," Wes said.

"One of the main reasons I wanted you to be aware of what happened is because Rudy blamed you," Linda said.

"Me? What did I do?" Allyson wasn't shocked. Rudy always blamed others for his shortcomings.

"You did your job," Linda said. "It's apparent from everything that you did your job according to the regulations and requirements. Rudy didn't. He wanted to sabotage you."

"Because I'm a good worker?" Allyson was trying to wrap her head around it.

"Yes, also because you're a woman," Linda said. "You have nothing to worry about, Allyson."

"What about Starr Construction?" There was so much wrong there.

"I've asked one of the state inspectors to go out to their sites," Wes said. "We don't know how much Rudy falsified for them. We can only, at this time, prove what he did to Riggs Construction."

Allyson nodded. "If you need my help with anything, let me know." She was willing to help where she could.

"I'll keep your offer in mind." Wes nodded at her. "For now, go home. Monday is going to be soon enough to deal with all of this."

"Thanks, Wes, Linda." Allyson stood and left the room in shock. They'd actually fired Rudy. After shutting down her computer, she grabbed her stuff and drove home. By the time she got home, her head pounded like someone was inside with a hammer trying to break out.

Damn. She didn't need this tonight. She took two painkillers, then found an outfit for tonight and put it in a bag. Shoes. She found a pair of low heels that she could survive a night in.

She pulled up to Zeke's house right at five. His truck sat in the driveway. Allyson took a deep breath. The painkillers had taken the edge off her headache, but that was about it.

Buck up. She'd survive. It wasn't the first time she'd gone out with a headache. Grabbing her bag, she walked up to his front door. She wasn't going to ruin tonight by talking about what happened at work or her headache. Tonight was for them.

* * * *

"I need to review the rules for Wicked Sanctuary," Zeke said as he drove.

"Rules?"

"Yep. Max created a place where people would feel safe in their sexuality and in the lifestyle."

"That sounds nice." She rubbed her forehead.

"Since you've seen the plans, you know there are bathrooms. There will be lockers inside for you to put your belongings in. No phones or anything are allowed on the floor."

"I can deal with that."

"I called Max about the dress code. Whatever you wear for tonight will be fine. Max waived it for you for tonight only since this was kind of spur of the moment."

"Oh?" Her voice held surprise. "I think I should be okay."

"I'm sure you will be. Submissives usually wear a light blouse, or a bra, or corset, or nothing. Skirt, shorts, a thong, or nothing. You can wear heels, ballet slippers, as the ladies call them, or go barefoot."

It was a good thing he remembered all these things. It was part of his job as a DM to alert Max or Jordan or Damon, which ever one of them was in the club on a given night, and escort the person out of the club with an explanation.

"Barefoot... That doesn't seem sanitary or safe."

"The club flooring is specially made and sanitized every night. The club isn't wall-to-wall bodies. We're busy, but we keep it within the fire code." That was one thing he made sure of, not that Ralph didn't. The club receptionist/sometimes bouncer was very good at his job.

He pulled up to the gate and input the code. The gate swung open, and he drove through. There were already several cars in the lot, a little surprising since it was only seven forty-five. Zeke helped Allyson from his truck, grabbed their bags, and they walked inside.

"Oh good, you're here," Dani jumped up and ran over to them. She hugged Allyson.

Zeke glanced at Ralph. "This is Allyson. Max

cleared her."

"He did." Ralph typed on the computer. "If you'll both sign in here, and here's your band." Ralph handed him a purple and white wristband. Zeke hesitated before he took it. "Master Max said it was appropriate."

Leave it to Max to think of these things. Zeke signed his name, then Dani told Allyson to sign hers. Zeke handed Allyson her bag.

"We'll be out shortly." Dani took Allyson's hand and pulled her into the ladies' room.

Zeke chuckled. The look an Allyson's face was pure confusion.

* * * *

"Dani, slow down," Allyson told her friend as she pulled her into the bathroom. Whoa! This was more like…she didn't know what. Showers lined one wall; another held lockers. There were towels and robes by the showers and benches to sit on. And down beyond the showers were the lavatories.

"I'm so happy you came tonight. Why didn't I know about it until I saw the guest list?"

"Sorry. It was a spur of the moment type of thing."

"It's okay." Dani pulled her over to the lockers. "Let's get you changed, and you can put everything in here."

"How?" The door to the locker was shut.

"Oh sorry. Put your thumb on the display." Allyson did and there was a series of three beeps and the door popped open. "When you close it, hold your thumb there again, and it will lock."

"Wow." This was super nice. Allyson picked up her bag and looked around.

"You can change in one of the bathroom stalls or in the shower."

Allyson chose the shower, she pulled the curtain and started stripping. Dani kept talking as she changed clothes. When she came out, she was in a short black skirt with a midnight-blue halter-top and one-inch heels.

"Does this work?"

"You're going to knock Zeke's socks off."

Warmed by Dani's response, Allyson dropped her bag in the locker. "Thanks. I'm glad I had something suitable." She shut the locker and, three beeps later, walked out of the ladies' room with Dani. Zeke was waiting.

Dani glanced at Zeke, then grinned knowingly at Allyson. "I need to get back to work. See you inside. Later."

Allyson couldn't keep her eyes off of Zeke. Her breath caught in her throat. He was wearing a pair of black pants that rode low on his hips, no shirt, and black loafers. Her insides melted into a puddle of goo.

"This is for you." His voice was husky. He placed a purple and white wristband on her.

"What is this for?"

"All club members wear these, it lets the Doms know the availability of the sub and their experience level. In this case, you're taken and a novice."

"Taken, am I?"

"You bet you are." He snagged her around the waist and drew her to him. "A few more things before we go in. If you see black and yellow that's a dungeon monitor." He pointed to his wristband. "Remember, you're going to see a lot of people you probably know in there."

She repeated what she'd read in the NDA. "No talking outside the club about who's in the club."

"Right. Now I have to work from eight until ten, then midnight to two. So I'm going to put you in the green area. It's where subs wait and talk."

"Okay. Are there any rules about who I can talk to?" The play parties sometimes had very strict rules regarding protocol.

"You can talk to anyone; just remember the right form of address. Doms shouldn't bother you at all."

"All right."

"Once I get off at ten, I'll show you around."

"I'll be fine, Zeke."

"Yes, you're safe here." He put his arm around her waist and guided her into the club.

The first thing Allyson noticed was the lighting: subtle, but also bright enough she could see everything. Then there was the music. It wasn't so loud people couldn't talk, yet enough in the background that it could still be heard.

"There's a bar?" That surprised her.

"Water, juice, and soft drinks only. Max doesn't permit alcohol unless it's a special occasion." Zeke led her farther into the club. There were people milling around. He guided her over to an area with a group of sofas where several women were sitting.

"Hi, Allyson," Sierra jumped up and came over to them. "Sir," Sierra turned to Zeke. "You're working tonight, right? I'll take care of her."

Zeke nodded. "I'll see you in a couple of hours. If you need anything, ask one of the women." He drew her in for a kiss.

Allyson couldn't help herself. She wrapped her arms around his neck as they kissed. When they parted, it took her a minute to get her breath back. She watched Zeke walk away with a grin on her face.

"Well, damn," a female voice muttered.

"Allyson," Sierra started. "This is Crystal and Tessa." She indicated the two women sitting on the sofa together.

Crystal's hair was reddish-brown, pulled back, and her green eyes glowed with excitement. Tessa had a lighter shade of hair, and her dark eyes were serious.

"It's very nice to meet you both," Allyson said with a smile.

"We're glad you're here." Sierra led her over to an unoccupied sofa. "As you know, I'm engaged to Max," Sierra said, waving to where the men were gathered, talking.

"Jordan's my man. He's on the right of Max."

"And Damon is on the left. He's mine, and if you need any toys, just ask. He can make you anything you want."

Allyson started coughing. "Are you okay?" Sierra asked.

She nodded. "Makes toys?" The words were rough coming from her lips.

"Oh yes. Sorry, I forgot you're new. Along with owning Kleinman's, Damon makes adult toys." Tessa tilted her head. "Wait, you were at the bookstore opening with Dani."

"I was."

"Did you like it?" Tessa asked.

"The bookstore? Yes, it's very nice."

"Have you gone into the adult side yet?" Crystal asked.

Heat filled Allyson's face. "Yes, not at all what I expected." It was true.

"A lot of people say that," Tessa commented.

"Oh, look, Lara is here." Sierra jumped up and drew another woman over. "Lara, this is Allyson."

"Hey, Allyson." Lara smiled. "Why am I not surprised to see you here?"

"Maybe because all our men seem to drag their women here," Sierra said.

Allyson tilted her head. "Drag?"

"Sierra, don't scare the poor girl off," Crystal said. "She doesn't mean it literally."

Allyson's muscles relaxed.

"Lara, I wanted to ask you if you knew of a meeting place we can use?" Sierra asked as Lara sat down.

"For what?" Lara asked.

"That one never explains." Crystal waved her hand at Sierra. "The guys want to create meeting groups, one for the Doms and another for the subs so we can discuss stuff that pertains to us and get advice without interference from know-it-all Doms."

"Ohhh." Lara's eyes brightened. "That would be so helpful for those of us new to the lifestyle. If you do it on Sundays, I could host it at the café."

"I don't want to put you out on your day off," Sierra said.

"It's okay. I won't do anything big, just drinks and some finger food. I'd love to have it at the café. It's private and there's plenty of parking."

"What do you think, Allyson?" Crystal asked.

Allyson froze. "I'm sort of new to the lifestyle, but I think having a place where subs can talk and ask questions would be a good idea." It was a fantastic idea. It would help her understand better, and she was sure it would help others too.

"Lara, I want to pay for the food," Sierra sad.

Lara started to shake her head.

"What if all the subs chipped in each week?" Allyson suggested; it would make her feel better if she could contribute something. "This way no one person would bear the cost, and sharing the expenses would make everyone feel like they were a part of the group."

"That's a great idea," another woman said as she sat down on another sofa with another woman.

"Hi, Regina, Harper," Sierra said. "This is Allyson, Zeke's sub. Allyson, Regina and Harper; they're what we call club subs." Sierra waved her hand at the two women.

"What she means is that we're not attached to a

Dom; we play with who we want to," Regina said.

"I love this idea of us subs meeting. I know there are things I still have questions about and don't want to talk to a Dom about," Harper said.

The women all looked at each other, and in that instant, a bond formed.

"That's it. Everyone will have an equal voice in the group. Brilliant, Allyson," Sierra said.

"The expansion of the café is done, so we can use that space," Lara said.

"How does a week from Sunday sound to hold the first one? That will give me time to talk with the other subs," Sierra said.

"We can help," the others chimed in.

"We have the best group here." Sierra smiled. "For those of you who don't know, Allyson works at the code enforcement office." She turned to Allyson. "Can you tell us about your job?"

* * * *

"How are things going with Allyson?" Max asked when Zeke joined them after his first shift was done. Damon had walked off to do his shift with Colby.

"Good." He'd talked to Max off and on about Allyson, being pretty general, but Max had given him some ideas.

"I'd say it's going well since you got her here," Jordan said.

"Yeah."

"They've been in a deep discussion for a while now; I wonder what they're talking about?" Zeke asked. He glanced over at the women. He'd been

200

checking in on Allyson visually as he worked. She was relaxed, laughing and talking with the women. That made him happy.

"Probably the sub meetings," Max said.

"Sub meetings?" Zeke asked. It sounded interesting.

"It was something we discussed a while back," Jordan said. "Damon had read about them. The concept is the Doms have their own group where they talk with other Doms about anything and everything with no repercussions. The same should go for the subs."

"I've been told there are some things a sub can't or maybe won't ask their Dom," Max said.

Zeke frowned. Did Allyson feel that way? He told her she could ask him anything.

"I think the subs feel better talking with other subs, especially the women," Jordan chimed in.

"That's true," Zeke rubbed his chin.

"All right, I think it's time I steal my lady away for some play time." Max broke away from the group and walked over to the women. He took Sierra's hand, pulled her to her feet, and led her away from group as Sierra laughed.

Zeke followed. He held his hand out to Allyson. "Shall we walk around?"

"Yes...Sir." She'd hesitated, but it didn't bother him. It wasn't second nature to her yet.

He grinned at her as she placed her hand in his, and he drew her up into his arm. "Ladies," he nodded to the other subs and led Allyson away.

"As you can see, we have areas where we can sit and talk with others. Plus the green area for the subs, where you were sitting."

"It was so nice to be able to talk with others," she said.

"Over here, we have the scene stations." He waved his hand. "We have all sorts. I'm sure the St. Andrews Cross and spanking benches are familiar."

"They are, Sir. I've seen them at parties."

"We have a wide variety of spanking benches, some massage tables, and bondage tables. We also have a modular bondage system and what most of us call the spider web."

She glanced to where he was pointing and shivered before she rubbed her temple.

"What's wrong?" he asked. Why hadn't he noticed the slight tightening around her eyes before?

"A headache. I thought it was gone, but it's come back." She massaged her forehead.

"Why didn't you say anything?" Zeke didn't like that she was hurting and hadn't told him.

"Because I thought it was gone. It wasn't as bad when I was taking with everyone, but now it's back with a vengeance."

Zeke frowned. "Come with me." He led her to an empty massage table. "Sit here for a minute."

"All right." Allyson sat on the stage while Zeke went across the room. He returned with several towels, a blanket, a bottle of water, and small bottle. He mounted the stage, and put everything on the small table, before returning to her. He took her hand

and helped her onto the stage.

"Zeke...Sir?"

There was a slight tremor in her voice.

"Easy, sweetheart." He kept his tone soft. "I'm going to give you a massage to help relieve the headache." Zeke guided her over to the massage table. "Lie face down."

Allyson did as he asked.

"I'm going to use bergamot oil, which has a lemony aroma. It will help with a headache."

"All right, Sir."

He made sure Allyson was positioned properly before he swept her hair over her shoulder and out of the way. "Are you okay with me undoing your halter-top?"

"Yes, Sir."

Zeke undid the fastening and let it fall, then he grabbed the oil, poured some in is palm, and rubbed his hands together.

He ran his palms over her back up to her shoulders. She was tense; this wasn't good. Zeke curved his fingers over her shoulders and massaged.

"Oh, that feels so good."

Zeke continued, then began to massage the base of her neck. Allyson groaned. He was on the right track. Zeke tunneled his fingers under her hair to her scalp, then back to her neck and shoulders.

With each pass of his hands, her muscles loosened. Zeke continued until she was putty under his touch.

"How's the headache?" he asked softly.

"Gone." Her voice was quiet and drowsy.

"Good." Grabbing one of the towels, he wiped off his hands, then used the other one to rub over her back and shoulders. Then he refastened her halter-top. "Lay there until you feel like moving."

"That could be never."

Zeke laughed softly. "I'll be right here." He cleaned up everything and motioned Harper over.

"Harper, if you would please put the oil back and put these towels in the basket."

"Of course, Sir."

He turned to see Allyson on her side, watching him. He grinned. After grabbing the blanket, he helped Allyson sit up on the massage table and placed the blanket over her shoulders.

"I don't think I need it," she said.

"Keep it on for a few minutes. And here." He handed her the bottle of water after twisting off the cap. "Drink, you need to hydrate."

She took several swallows. "That was absolutely wonderful. Thank you."

"You don't have to thank me." He brushed a kiss over her forehead. "Next time, tell me if you're not feeling well."

"Yes, Sir. I didn't want to ruin our night."

"The only thing that would do that is you not being open with me."

Allyson looked down at the floor, but Zeke didn't want her to hide. "Look at me, please." Her gaze met his. "I understand how you don't like to rely on others. Your independence is one of the reasons I'm attracted to you. I wouldn't have canceled us coming here tonight, but at least I would have known you had a headache and could have helped stave it off."

"That's true. I'll make sure next time to tell you, Sir."

"You better." He helped her off the table and down into the aftercare area. "Sit there, finish up your water, and relax. I'll be right back."

Zeke cleaned off the massage table with sterile wipes and returned to Allyson. She'd finished her bottle of water. Good. He sat down beside her and pulled her to his side. "Want to tell me about the tension headache?"

She tilted her head. "How did…"

"The tension in your muscles. Also, the minute I touched your neck, it was like I'd hit a nerve, and you sighed."

"That felt so good."

"I bet it did. So what caused it? In all the time we've known each other, I've never seen you that tense."

She sighed. "Rudy was fired today."

Zeke jerked in surprise. "Why didn't you tell me?"

"I didn't want to talk about work and ruin our night."

"But it gave you a headache?"

"Sort of. It was dramatic, to say the least. I was pulled into a private meeting with my boss and the head of HR."

This didn't sound good. "Are you in trouble?"

"No. Good news is I have all your jobs back."

"Thank god for small favors. But won't that mean you'll get all of Starr Construction jobs as well?"

"Not at the moment. I can't say any more than that."

"I get it." He hugged her close to his side. "Want to watch a scene? I've got about forty-five minutes before my next shift."

"Yes, please." Zeke helped her to her feet, and Allyson held the blanket. "What shall I do with this?"

"See the big basket over there? Throw it in. It will be cleaned."

"Okay." She hurried over and dropped the blanket in, then was back at his side. "Before we go to watch, I have a question."

"Go ahead."

"At the parties, there were sometimes women who walked around in body paint; does that happen here?"

"No." Zeke trailed his fingers over her arm. "Max is very particular about what activities he allows in the club."

"Why?"

"Safety, for one." He lifted his hand to play with her hair.

"You like doing that."

"What?"

"Playing with my hair. You do it all the time."

"I do. It's soft and silky, like your skin."

Allyson ducked her head.

"None of that, sweetheart." He cupped her jaw

and lifted her face to his. "You're a beautiful woman. By the way, I love what you're wearing."

"Thank you." She cleared her throat. "Here I see DMs like you paying attention so things don't get out of control, and I don't see anything I would classify as dangerous."

"Like what?"

"Needle play, fire play. Heck, at some of the parties, I've seen machines that simulate sex with a person." A tremor went through her body.

"Fire play is allowed, but only at certain times, and all precautions are taken. No needle play. And as for the type of machines you're talking about, Max doesn't allow them. They can be dangerous, especially if you don't understand how they work."

"The club is busier now."

"It's almost midnight. We usually start hopping around eleven, then it starts to die down around two, but sometimes later with all the new members."

"You mentioned that. Why so many new members?"

"The club has become more popular since Damon and Tessa's press conference."

"I remember that." She glanced up at him. "I was kind of surprised they outted the club like that."

"They didn't. Max and Jordan were well aware of what was going to happen."

"Jordan? How does he fit into this?"

"Jordan and Damon are partners with Max in the club."

"Oh, I thought Max owned it."

"The three of them came together to make the club what it is today." He leaned closer. "Max is the majority owner from what I understand, but Jordan and Damon are involved."

"Nice." Zeke led her to a bondage scene and found them a spot to sit. He tucked her close to his side. "If you have any questions, ask."

"Okay." She rested her head on his shoulder.

Zeke held her close, hoping that, when she was comfortable, maybe they could play in the club.

* * * *

It was close to two-thirty in the morning when Zeke pulled up to his house. He glanced over at his sleeping passenger. Allyson had done great at the club. While he was giving her that massage, several people stopped to watch, and she never said a word. Then they watched a bondage scene until he had to go back to his DM duties. She'd made friends with the subs, and he was happy to see her smiling and chatting.

Zeke quietly got out of his truck, opened the front door, then gathered Allyson into his arms. She stirred as he shut the front door. Zeke hesitated in the hallway. Take her to guest room or his room?

Her sleepy voice reached his ears. "Sleep with you."

"Are you sure?" He didn't want to take advantage of her. Yes, they'd played some in his home and had sex, but they hadn't slept in the same bed together all night.

"Please. I want to be with you." Her eyes were

drowsy, but there was determination there as well.

He turned and carried her into his bedroom. He'd left his shutters open so there was enough moonlight for him to see where he was going. The sound of her shoes hitting the floor made him smile as he placed her in the middle of the bed before he stripped.

When he glanced at Allyson, she was watching him, her gaze filled with desire and need. She held out her hand, and he climbed onto the mattress.

"Are you sure about this?" He'd been taking things at a slow pace.

"Yes." She scooted closer to him. "I want you, Zeke. Only you."

He reached up and cupped her cheek. "I want you too."

"Good." She lifted her hands and released her halter-top, allowing it to fall.

Lord, he loved her breasts. Full, with pink nipples. He enjoyed playing with them. When she wiggled in an attempt to sit up, he stopped her.

"Let me." He helped her sit up and pulled the halter-top over her head, then reached for the skirt. Within seconds, it joined her top wherever he threw them. He traced her black thong. "I never pictured you wearing a thong."

"Uncomfortable things." She wiggled.

"Then let me make you comfortable." He whisked the offending scrap of material away. "Better?"

"Much." Her arms wound around his neck.

Zeke lowered his head and captured her lips with his. Tonight was for her.

* * * *

Allyson's tongue toyed with Zeke's as he kissed her. She needed this man like she needed no other. Tonight had sealed them together. Of course, he wasn't aware of that yet. Allyson hadn't actually made the connection until she was sitting and talking with some of the subs while Zeke did his second shift.

He'd been so worried about her when she said she had a headache. She'd kept it to herself because she didn't want to ruin their night at the club, but he'd figured it out. The massage had been heavenly, but not only that.

The way Zeke held and cared for her. She'd never had that in her life. This man was a keeper. Yeah, he'd wormed his way into her heart over the past months. Him being into kink was a nice bonus. But tonight wasn't about kink; it was about them as a couple.

His lips trailed from hers to her breasts. She arched into his touch as he took one nipple in his mouth. Lord, the things this man could do with his lips. He teased her constantly, and when he'd used those talented lips on her pussy, she'd never come so hard.

He loved her body and took care of her without being overbearing. He respected her personally and professionally. He was also genuine and lacking any pretense. Was it any wonder she was falling in love with him? She stiffened.

"Are you okay?" Zeke's husky voice sent shivers of awareness through her.

"I'm fine." She slid her fingers into his hair.

"You're so handsome and all mine."

"That I am." He lowered his head.

When had she fallen for Zeke? She wasn't sure. But she knew it was love; she'd never felt this way for any man. A nip on her hip broke her out of her thoughts.

"Where is your mind wandering off to?"

"Thinking about you." It was the truth.

"Good." He slid between her thighs, his cock nudging her pussy. "I can't wait any longer to have you."

His eyes were blazing with passion and need. Allyson curved her arms around him, widened her legs, and lifted her hips.

He thrust. A moan left her lips as he stretched her.

"You feel so good," he whispered.

"You do too." He did. Her muscles stretched to accommodate him, and it felt wonderful. Her legs encircled his hips, and he groaned.

"Woman, you're going to kill me." He slid out and back in.

"I think I'm going to combust." Her toes tingled, and a familiar tightening started in her belly.

"So fucking beautiful." His lips captured hers. Their tongues tangled, retreated, tasted each other as he thrust.

Allyson's nerves shimmied to their own beat as Zeke made love to her. Her hands roamed over his back, her nails lightly scraping over his skin.

When he finally released her mouth, she gulped in air. "More," she whispered.

"As you wish." He took her right nipple in his mouth and bit the taut peak lightly before switching to the left one.

"I'm not going to last."

"Come for me, my Allyson. Let me feel you let go."

She took a breath, and her orgasm crashed over her. Her pussy tightened around his cock, wanting more of him. Zeke was still pumping away when the tremors started to subside, and then they started again.

This time, he went over the edge with her. His essence filled her with warmth and caused another small climax. The next thing she knew, Zeke rolled onto his back with her on top as more tremors rolled through their bodies.

Allyson rested her cheek against his chest, listening to his rapid heartbeat. She did this to him. A smile overtook her lips.

"I can feel that satisfied smile." His voice was raspy.

"I am very satisfied, thank you." She wanted to laugh. Zeke did that to her. Pulled her out of her head.

"Me too." He shifted them, allowing his cock to slip free.

Allyson instantly missed having him in her. She tilted her head, took one of his nipples into her mouth, and bit. His cock jumped against her leg.

"Someone is still frisky." Zeke slapped her ass.

"The night is young."

Zeke laughed, put his hands on her waist, and

lifted her until his cock was free. Allyson braced her hands on his shoulders. He reached over, grabbed some tissues, and wiped himself off, tossing the tissues away. "Put me in you."

She reached down and grasped his cock. He was hard again. Zeke lowered her as she held him until the head breached her pussy, then lowered her farther.

"Oh my god, this feels so good. So different." She couldn't describe the sensations flowing through her body. It was more than nerve endings coming to life. It was like a light switch had been flipped on, and the voltage was too high.

"Ride me, sweetheart."

"Anything you say."

Chapter 9

Allyson woke to bright sunshine flowing into the bedroom. Wait. Her bedroom faced west not east. Zeke's. Her lips turned up into a smile. She'd spent the night with Zeke after they'd been to the club. Pure happiness filled her heart.

"Good morning." His gruff voice caused her smile to widen.

"Morning. What time is it?" She covered her mouth as she yawned. The last time she'd looked at the clock, it was around five.

"Almost ten."

She hummed. "I don't want to move."

"Nothing says we have to." His palm skimmed up and down her back.

"True." She stretched against his body. "But I need a shower." As much as she hated to get up, she felt sticky after all their lovemaking last night.

"I do too." Zeke sat up with a yawn.

"Okay." She slid her legs off the mattress. "Last one to the shower loses." She took off toward his bathroom.

"Hey." His bellow made her laugh.

She barely beat him into the bathroom, but it

hadn't been a fair race, not that he complained.

"What is my penalty since I lost?" he asked.

"Me." She'd never felt so free with a man as she did with Zeke. She could be playful or serious. He'd take all sides of her.

"Oh good. Let's play." He flipped on the water, then scooped her up and set her inside the big shower before stepping in behind her.

* * * *

The next week was hectic. Picking up all of Rudy's work and her own kept Allyson busy from the time she got into the office until the end of her shift. The upside was she was seeing Zeke every day.

Wes already told her he was interviewing to see which of the two junior inspectors he wanted to move up—one to take Rudy's place and the other to help out when needed. Allyson had never felt so happy. She walked into Sweet and Savory on Friday afternoon to see Dani waiting for her.

"If your smile gets any bigger, you'll need a new face," Dani said, giving her a hug.

"I'm happy to see you." Allyson sat down.

"More like Zeke is making you happy."

"He is." She was happy, and Zeke did that to her. But he wasn't happy when she begged off breakfast with him at his parents last Sunday. He'd asked her several times, but each time she found an excuse. When she was growing up rumors had run rampant. Both Dani and her grandmother had sat Allyson down and told her she didn't need to worry about them. It was her parents' neglect that people were most upset about, but none of them would do anything about it.

Dani's grandmother quietly told Allyson she'd tried once to talk with Allyson's parents but were met with indifference and distain. So instead, she concentrated on making sure Allyson had a safe place to go whenever she wanted.

"I'm so glad," Dani said. "So Sunday, we set up the sub meeting for four in the afternoon."

"Cool." Allyson was happy to be involved with the group.

"My turn to get lunch. Your usual?" Dani asked.

"Yes, please." Allyson put a reminder in her phone about the meeting. She'd just put her phone away when Zeke's sister, Josie, sat down. What was with this girl and stealing empty seats?

"Josie, good to see you again. But my friend will return in a minute."

"Hopefully, this will just take a minute. Why won't you come to breakfast at my parents' house?"

Allyson was taken back. Yes, Josie was direct, but she hadn't expected that. "It's none of your business." Allyson fought down the panic filling her veins. What was Zeke's family saying about her? Did Josie know about her past? Would her continued pushing off meeting his family drive a wedge between her and Zeke?

"I like you, Allyson, but my parents are beginning to wonder if there is something wrong because you refuse to visit."

Allyson took a deep breath. It seemed that Josie

didn't have any information on her past at this point. "Josie, I know you mean well, but my reasons are mine."

"That's what I wondered. Zeke won't say much. This is hurting him, and I don't like that my brother is hurt."

"What?" This was the first she heard of this. She never intended to hurt Zeke in any way. Her gut tightened.

"I see it in his face each Sunday when he explains that you're not coming. Allyson, I love my brother, but if you're going to keep locking him out like this, then please break it off."

"I don't think that's your place to ask," Dani said, standing next to Josie.

Josie looked up. "I don't want to see my brother in pain." Josie stood and left.

Dani sat down, and Allyson stared at her friend for a long moment before hiding her face in her hands. "She's right."

"No, she's not." Dani placed her hands on the table. "Your relationship is growing and changing. Meeting the parents is a big step. I can understand why you're reluctant. Your parents were lousy role models, true. And yeah, their rep wasn't the best. People weren't nearly as accepting then of alternative lifestyles as they might be today. But most people — at least those who are worth knowing — aren't going to hold you responsible for what your parents may have done."

Allyson snorted. "I know, Dani. It's hard to shake

the damage they did when I was kid." While her parents made sure there was food in the house, and Allyson had a roof over her head, that was it. It was like Allyson didn't exist the rest of the time. "But the last thing I want to do is hurt Zeke."

"His sister is seeing what she wants to see. Trust me. Zeke would tell you if there's an issue. Remember, one of the things about a D/s relationship is communication."

"Yeah." But would he? Allyson wasn't so sure. The few times he tried bringing up her childhood, she'd shut him down. Hard.

"Now, tell me more about last weekend. We've barely had a chance to talk."

* * * *

Allyson pulled up to Zeke's house at eleven on Saturday, still thinking about Josie's bombshell last week. She hadn't had the guts to ask Zeke about it. Heck, they'd barely seen each other this past week, between her job and his.

There was another car parked in front, so she parked behind his truck. She wondered who he had visiting him as she rang the doorbell.

Zeke opened the door. His hair was disheveled. "Thank goodness." He grasped her by the shoulders. "Save me."

Before she could ask him what he needed saving from, an older woman came bustling up. Her brown hair framed her face, and her dark eyes made Allyson think she could see all the way into one's soul.

"Ah, you must be, Allyson." She elbowed Zeke

out of the way, then she framed Allyson's face with surprisingly strong hands. "So pretty." She kissed both of Allyson's cheeks.

Allyson blinked, not sure what to do, but she didn't have to guess who this was. Zeke had his mother's eyes. "Hello, Mrs. Riggs."

Zeke's mother made a tsking sound. "Violetta, dear." She looked at her son. "Do you always leave your women standing on the threshold?"

He looked up as if praying for patience. "I was about to invite Allyson in when you came running up and pushed me out of the way."

"Pshaw." His mother waved her hands in an exasperated gesture. "Come in. Quincy will want to meet you."

Allyson glanced at Zeke as his mother grabbed her hand and pulled her into the house and toward the family room.

"One moment, please." Allyson slid off her shoes.

"So polite." Violetta stared at Zeke.

Allyson fought not to laugh at the contrite look on Zeke's face. Is this how families acted?

"Come, please." Violetta pulled her down the hall into the family room with Zeke following. When they entered, an older gentleman stood up, his dark hair tinted with gray and his dark eyes twinkling.

This is how Zeke would look as he aged. Not bad at all. "Mr. Riggs, I'm Allyson." She held her hand out to him.

"Call me Quincy, my dear." He took her hand and squeezed it.

"She has such warm manners, not like this one." She waved her hands at Zeke. "Has he brought any women home to meet us?"

"Maybe because you'd scare them off," Zeke muttered.

Allyson hid a grin. Zeke's tone was playful, not angry.

"Come sit down." Violetta pulled her toward the sofa, but luckily Allyson was able to maneuver herself to the big soft chair. She could imagine being between Violetta and her husband. Too close. She needed space to take this all in.

"Do you want something to drink, Allyson?" Zeke asked.

"Beer, please." She wanted something stronger. Maybe later, after his parents left. If she survived.

"I'll have coffee dear, and so will your father."

Quincy was shaking his head, and Zeke laughed. "Be right back."

Allyson wasn't sure how she felt about being alone with his parents, but then she wasn't alone. With the open floor plan, Zeke could see and hear them from the kitchen.

"So Allyson, how long have you known our son?" Violetta asked.

Allyson nibbled at her lower lip. "I've known Zeke since right after he started his construction company."

Violetta's eyes widened and laughter floated from the kitchen. "This is no laughing matter, young man." She glared at her son. "You've known each other for over four years, and we're just now finding out about her?"

"Mom, think about how you phrased the question. Yes, Allyson and I have known each other professionally for that long. We recently started seeing each other on a personal basis." Zeke carried in two mugs and handed one to his mother, the other to his father, who took a quick sip.

"Thank you, son," his father said with a grin.

"You work in construction, Allyson?" Violetta asked.

"No, ma'am." Allyson took the mug of beer from Zeke with a smile. He knew she'd drink direct from the can or bottle, so it must be because of his parents that he poured a mug for her. "I work for the city."

"Which is how we met," Zeke said, taking the chair across from Allyson.

"What took you so long to ask her out?" His mother admonished him. "She's a beautiful woman. Why did you dally around? She could have married someone else while you waited to make up your mind."

Allyson choked on a sip of beer at Violetta's words.

"Now, Violetta," Quincy started. "Don't scare Allyson off with talk like that."

Zeke's mother sat back with a huff and stared at her son. "You are to bring her to breakfast tomorrow."

Zeke stared at Allyson, and she glanced at his parents, who were talking to each other. She raised her hand to her face, enough to hide her profile from his parents, and stuck her tongue out at him. A smile overtook his lips. "Maybe you should ask Allyson."

Violetta turned her attention back to her, and Allyson sighed. Yes, she had been making up excuses not to go. But what choice did she have now? This wasn't an easy decision for her.

Allyson glanced at Zeke, who was staring at her with a knowing look. She squirmed in her seat. She wasn't about to break his mother's heart. "Of course he's bringing me. I wouldn't miss it."

"Very good." Violetta clapped her hands as if she'd accomplished what she came to do.

"Honey, we should be going and let these two kids do whatever they were planning," Quincy said, standing up.

Allyson's face turned hot, and she knew she was blushing to the roots of her hair. Zeke chuckled, and she wrinkled her nose at him.

"Of course." Violetta stood.

Zeke and Allyson followed suit, and they all trooped to the front door, saying their goodbyes. She and Zeke stood in the open doorway until his parents' car was out of sight.

"Zeke, did you have to throw me under the bus? Really?" Allyson stomped back into the house. Without shoes on, her steps didn't make much noise. She was angry at Zeke and at herself as well. Now she was committed to breakfast tomorrow with his parents.

Her tummy cramped. What if they asked about her parents? Her childhood? How much could she get away with not saying? Why did it matter so much? She didn't have to talk about it unless she wanted to.

"You're upset. And you've been tense since you got here. What aren't you telling me, Allyson?"

She flopped down on the sofa and deflected. She was good at deflecting. "Do they often surprise you like that?" It had been a little unsettling to her that Zeke hadn't tried to call her to say his parents were there, but then again, it looked like they'd arrived right before she did. Cut the man some slack, he couldn't control his parents.

"No. I suspect my sister had a hand in it."

Allyson crossed her arms over her chest. Josie. She should have figured that out after their little confrontation the other day. "I hope I passed muster." Her insides were churning.

"You did fine." Zeke sat down next to her. "What has you so spooked?" He ran his fingers over her arm.

Zeke was too darn observant. "I told you my parents were pretty self-absorbed. That's enough to spook anyone."

"You are not your parents," Zeke said.

"God, I hope not."

"Then there's no reason to worry. My parents, if you hadn't noticed, are pretty laid back."

Allyson laughed. "Your mother is a force to be reckoned with."

"That's a half-Italian mother for you. And we were talking about you, not my mother. Why is the idea of Sunday brunch bothering you?"

"Because I don't know how to act. So what are we

doing today?" Allyson asked, steering the conversation away from her parents.

"Just be yourself."

She could see he wanted to push the issue, and she held his gaze, resolute. He tapped the side of his leg several times, then stopped and reached for her hand. Allyson knew the discussion wasn't over by a long shot, but he'd apparently decided to let it go. For now. "I thought today we could do some intricate Shibari, if you're up for it."

"Really?" Zeke had done some ties on her. Basic Shibari ties, but he hadn't tried any heavy rope bondage on her yet.

"Yes. It will be minor. I'm curious how you'll react since you took to the basics like a duck to water."

"Cool. Where are we going to do this?" Thank goodness she'd only had a sip or two of beer.

"Bedroom. I set everything up this morning."

Allyson stood. "I'm ready, Sir."

"Go undress, and I'll be right there."

She all but ran down the hallway to his bedroom, thoughts of family and brunches gone as excitement flowed through her. She was finally going to experience rope bondage.

* * * *

Zeke strode into his bedroom with a heavy heart. Not because of wanting to do Shibari on Allyson, but how she avoided his questions. Her worries about not knowing how to act with his parents puzzled him. He shook off his worries. To do what he wanted, he needed focus and concentration.

Allyson had already removed her clothes. His woman's body was perfect. "Stand in the middle of the room please." He was glad his master bedroom was big; it gave him plenty of room to work. He glanced at Allyson as he crossed over to where he'd laid his supplies.

Zeke closed his eyes as he picked up the first bunch of nylon rope. He let the rope slide over his fingers, getting the feel for it. After taking several deep breaths, he centered himself, before going over to Allyson.

"I won't be as talkative as I am usually, so ask any questions."

"Yes, Sir."

"Same as before, if anything starts to tingle or go numb, tell me right away. If anything doesn't feel right, tell me. You have your safe word."

"Yes, Sir. I'm ready."

He nodded and pulled the rope through his hands. The smoothness and strength of the rope flowed through his fingers and helped him center himself more. He worked the rope until he had a large loop, and he laid it over her neck with another loop hanging down over her chest.

He saw the trust and wonder in Allyson's eyes, and his confidence soared. The loop hanging down her chest was perfect. Taking the long ends of the rope he'd left hanging from the loop, he walked behind her. With each step, his breathing deepened, his heart settled into a steady beat, and his senses came alive.

Allyson was relaxed as he worked, her breathing soft, but increasing. There was a slight flush to her body. He continued with the ties, letting himself stroke her skin as he tied his rope around her.

The silky feel of her skin beneath his hands as he tied his rope into a bra harness made his nerves settle and his senses come alive. He glanced over her shoulder, making sure the rope was placed perfectly above and below her breasts. Zeke ran his fingers under the rope before he started doing an overhand knot with the rest of the rope.

When he was done, he stepped back, satisfied with his work. But so much more than that. Energy flowed between him and Allyson.

"How are you doing?" Zeke noted her breathing had increased, and her nipples were taut. She was getting aroused. Good. He'd hoped this would do that to her.

"Fine, Sir." She looked down. "Interesting bra, Sir."

Zeke grinned. "Are you okay standing? I can have you sit for the next piece."

"I'm okay, Sir."

"Good." Zeke picked up the next piece of rope and went to work. He'd put her in a chair in a bit.

* * * *

Allyson fought to stand still while Zeke was doing his rope bra. The sensation of his fingers against her skin and the way the rope caressed her skin sent shafts of pleasure through her body. They had done some basic Shibari, but this was so much more. She

226

wasn't sure how to explain it.

With each tie, her heart rate grew calmer, but her breathing was shorter. Excitement encased her entire being, along with curiosity at what Zeke was doing. Now, he held her right arm as he began wrapping it in a double strand of rope. She watched as he looped the rope around and around her arm until she had almost a rope glove. While the rope wasn't heavy, it felt like he was wrapping her up in his own little universe.

He lifted her arm. "Okay?" He checked each area that overlapped, making sure it wasn't tight against her skin.

"Fine, Sir. This is beautiful." She held up her arm and admired his work.

"Rope gauntlet. I'll do your other arm now."

Allyson watched Zeke work on her other arm. With each swipe of his fingers against her skin, her body temperature went up, and by the time he was done, she could barely stand still. When he stepped back, she shifted from one foot to the other and back again.

Her clit throbbed with need. She didn't understand it, but she was incredibly aroused, and he hadn't done anything blatantly sexual yet.

"You're having trouble standing still," he commented as he walked around her. His fingers trailed over her lower back, up her spine, over her shoulder, around to her neck, then down to the top of her breasts.

"Yes, Sir." Her breathing was choppy.

"Shibari can be deeply arousing," he said before

his lips captured one taut nipple.

Allyson's head fell back, and she arched into his mouth. His tongue bathed her nipple, and he bit it lightly before moving to the other. "Zeke…Sir."

He lifted his head and stared down at her. "A few more things first. But let's make you a bit more comfortable."

Zeke guided her over to a wide padded chair she hadn't noticed before and had her sit down. A shiver swept through her. What did he have planned now?

"Now, I'm going to tie your arms to the chair and then your legs." He picked up more rope and made quick work of tying her to the chair. Of course, he tied her with her legs open, and for good measure, put ropes above her knees.

"Are we still doing well?" He walked around, his fingers trailing over her skin once again.

"I'm fine, Sir. Why do you keep running your fingers over my skin?"

"To check to make sure I haven't cut off any circulation; cool skin would tell me that."

Allyson snorted. "I don't think I could be cold if I wanted to, Sir."

Zeke flashed her one of his sexy grins. "Now what shall I do with you?"

She squirmed under his gaze, but her pussy clenched with need. This man was a miracle to her. A man who understood her in life, and in pleasure. "Anything you want, Sir."

"Anything?" His eyebrows rose, then he grinned. "I think it's time I feasted on your body."

Zeke then showed her what he meant. It was a good thing he didn't have to be at Wicked Sanctuary until later that night.

* * * *

Allyson twisted her hands together in her lap as Zeke drove toward his parents' home Sunday morning.

"They don't bite," Zeke commented.

"I know." How could she explain? She never talked in detail to him about how she grew up. Shame flowed through her. There was no other word for it. She'd hidden a lot from friends when growing up. Not that rumors hadn't made the rounds.

Dani was one of the few people she'd told that her parents were swingers. Zeke would understand because he was in the lifestyle, but his parents might not. No, it was better if she kept this to herself.

Zeke pulled up in front of modest looking two-story home. The brown tones made the house feel warm and cozy. Allyson took a deep breath as they walked up the brick path to the front door.

"Zeke!" Josie yelled and came flying down the stairs.

Zeke dropped Allyson's hand to catch his sister in a hug.

"I've missed you," Josie said.

"You saw me a week ago."

"I know." Josie looked at her, and her eyes turned frosty. "Allyson."

"Josie." Josie's cold shoulder wasn't unexpected. Should she say she wasn't feeling well, call a ride share, and go?

Zeke let go of Josie and retook Allyson hands in his. His warmth sank into her bones. She'd do this for him.

They walked inside and took off their shoes before heading for the kitchen. Allyson blinked when they entered. His mother was fluttering around, but that wasn't what made her blink.

The kitchen was huge. The cherry wood cabinets glowed, along with the granite counters. Violetta stood at the center island that held a six-burner stove. Allyson glanced around. This was a chef's kitchen. A double oven, a refrigerator to die for, and lots of counter space. This was easily twice the size of Zeke's kitchen.

"Oh good, you're here," Violetta smiled. "Everything is almost ready."

"It smells wonderful," Allyson commented, and it did. She picked up hints of rosemary and Italian herbs.

"It should," Quincy said. "She's been up since seven trying to figure out what to cook.

"You didn't need to go to all that trouble," Allyson said.

Violetta waved her hands. "No trouble. Josie, is the table set?"

"Yes, Momma."

"Zeke, take Allyson in, and we'll bring in the food."

"Yes, Momma." He brushed a kiss over her cheek before leading Allyson into the dining room.

"Your mother went to a lot of trouble," she said softly.

"Momma loves to cook." Zeke pulled out a chair for her, and Allyson sat down. Within minutes, food was placed on the table. "My favorite." Zeke said. "There's an Italian sausage egg bake, then a frittata, fresh bread, cheese and fruit."

Allyson's mouth watered. Everything looked delicious.

"Coffee," Quincy said, bringing in two big carafes and small pitchers of milk and juice.

"*Buon appetito*," Violetta said.

Zeke picked up the frittata and handed it to Allyson. "Ladies first."

Allyson smiled as she took the plate and dished up a piece before handing it back to Zeke, who handed it to his mother.

With the first bite of the frittata, Allyson closed her eyes in bliss. Then came the Italian sausage egg bake. The slight spiciness of the sausage burst upon her tongue along with the taste of egg and fresh mozzarella cheese.

"I think I've died and gone to heaven," she said.

"Make sure to leave room for dessert," Violetta said.

"Dessert after breakfast?" That was something new to her.

"Not exactly dessert, but a breakfast pastry that Momma makes sure to bring out after we've eaten a healthy breakfast," Zeke said.

"Normally, we Italians are not big on breakfast,

but I learned with my men" — she gestured to Quincy and Zeke — "they needed good food in the morning. And so did my other son."

"You are a fantastic mother," Allyson said, and she meant it. Her mother rarely bothered. She'd learned how to get herself a bowl of cereal by the time she was four. Of course, there were times she'd made a mess, but she'd cleaned it up.

Sadness overcame her. How would her life have turned out if she'd had parents as supportive as Zeke's were? Would she be an inspector? Or doing something else?

Allyson shook her head. She'd learned not to look back at what could have been, but to deal with who she was today. But this day, it was more difficult to put things back in the box. They chatted about different things as they ate.

"Do you have any brother or sisters?" Quincy asked her.

"No. My parents never had another child after me." Which was a blessing in a way. Her parents hadn't been interested in raising her. A tremor went through her at the thought of having a brother or sister to deal with. She'd had a hard enough time making sure she was safe without the added responsibility.

"Do your parents live local?" Josie asked.

"They don't." Another small favor. After Allyson left home at eighteen, her parents decided to leave Pleasant Valley for the wilds of Montana. Apparently a friend of theirs owned land up there. It was funny that, once they left, she never heard from or saw any of their swinging friends again.

"That's a shame," Violetta said. "Do you get to see them often?"

Allyson shifted in her seat. How did she answer that one?

"Momma, no third degree, please," Zeke said.

"Then how will we get to know her?" Josie said, staring at Allyson.

Zeke opened his mouth, but Allyson squeezed his leg under the table. "It's okay, Zeke. No, I don't see them often. They live in Montana." She saw a gleam in Josie's eyes and wondered about it.

"More coffee?" Quincy asked.

"Yes, please." Allyson turned her attention to Violetta. "Tell me about your son, Ben. I understand he's in the military."

Violetta took the bait, and Allyson breathed a sigh of relief to have the attention off of her. She'd been a fool to think this would work. Zeke was from a loving, close family, where she had no one. Correction. She had Dani. Allyson suppressed a sigh.

* * * *

Three hours later, Zeke pulled up in front of his home. Allyson had been quiet on the drive. She held a platter of maritozzi in her lap. His mother insisted they take some of the sweet buns filled with whipped cream home with them.

They had a few hours before they were off to their respective Dom/sub meetings. This was the first one for both of them. Zeke liked the idea, because there were times, like now, he didn't know what to do.

Allyson was so quiet. He could tell she was worried and deeply thoughtful, but when he'd tried to ask her about it, she shut him down. He hadn't been happy with his sister.

Josie kept prodding Allyson about her childhood, even after their mother told her to stop. He was worried. His family could be a bit overwhelming.

"I'm sorry," Allyson whispered once they got inside his home and they'd taken off their shoes.

"For what?" He put the treat in the fridge and came back to find Allyson standing with her arms around her middle. Damn.

Zeke crossed over to her and pulled her into his arms. "What is scaring you?"

She shook her head but didn't step out of his embrace.

"Does my family scare you?"

"A bit."

At least she was talking. "I don't know why Josie was on such a kick about your childhood."

"She wants to make sure I'm good enough for her big brother." A tremor went through her body, and Zeke tightened his arms around her.

"You are more than good enough."

"Am I?" She leaned back in his embrace.

"Of course you are." How could she think otherwise? Something wasn't right here.

"I'm an only child. I have no idea what it means to have a brother or sister."

"That makes no difference to me. Besides I would

say you and Dani are sisters of the heart. Sometimes that's better than blood." He gazed down at her, but he could see the skepticism in those blue eyes. "Since I'm the oldest, do you know how many times I wanted to be an only child?"

She shook her head.

"Countless, but as we all grew up, there were advantages. We all have very different personalities."

"Your sister is like you. She wants to protect you, as you like to protect others."

"Maybe, but at times, she's driven to the point of ignoring everyone and everything else. And Ben, he loves the military. He likes being of service in some form, and that's his way of helping people."

"You are the responsible one, but not so much you don't know how to have fun."

"Guilty." He played with her hair. "I see you as someone who is trying to be tough but really wants someone to be there for her. Someone to belong to."

* * * *

Allyson stared at him as her heart pounded. How the hell had he figured that out? Oh, this was so not good. There was no way she was good enough for Zeke or his family. They deserved someone who had a childhood.

Not her, who grew up with swingers for parents, there was nothing wrong with them swinging, but neglecting her as a child was the problem. But for Allyson, sex was one thing, and making love should mean something. It did with Zeke. It meant a lot to her. Others wouldn't see it that way once they found out about her past. They'd have an issue with the neglect. Josie would take issue. For an enlightened young lady, she was acting immature. Zeke loved his sister. Heck, he was head over heels for his whole family. What would he do if he knew how screwed up her family was? She didn't know how to love. She was stupid to think she could have a relationship with Zeke. "I'm sorry," she whispered.

"Sweetheart," Zeke started.

"No, Zeke." She pushed against his chest, and he let her go. "You've had loving parents your whole life. You don't have any idea what it's like to be unwanted. You've never had to come to terms with the fact that your parents don't care about you. You don't know anything." She turned and hightailed it to the front door, pausing only long enough to grab her shoes and purse.

"Allyson!"

Zeke called her name, but she didn't look back. She fumbled to get her keys off the ring on her purse, finally opening her door with them still attached to her purse. She got in her truck, tossed her shoes and purse in the passenger seat before locking the doors.

"Allyson, sweetheart." Zeke's voice penetrated the glass. She ignored him and finally got her keys free. Jamming the key into the ignition, she turned the vehicle on.

"I'm sorry. I never meant to hurt you," she said, before backing down the driveway slowly. Zeke stood there with his mouth open. Tears welled in her eyes, but she refused to let them fall. Not until she got home. But she couldn't go home; Zeke would look for her there.

She turned onto the freeway. A couple exits later, unable to see because of the tears blurring her vision, she exited and pulled into a park. Allyson sat there clutching her belly, trying to find a way to stop the hurt. But there was no way to mitigate what she'd done.

Her entire body ached. What was she going to do now? She needed to clear her head. Pulling out her phone, she checked a special website she hadn't looked at in a long time. After inputting her member name and password, she found what she wanted. She was going to Seattle. She needed to lose herself at a party so the pain wouldn't find her. It was Sunday, and they'd party from noon until late tonight. And she knew she could lose herself there and hide her pain.

Chapter 10

Zeke stood in his driveway, dumbfounded, as Allyson drove away. What the hell happened? He jogged back into the house, found his keys, and slipped on his shoes. She had a head start on him, but that didn't matter.

Ten minutes later, he pulled into her apartment building parking lot. Her truck wasn't in its usual spot.

"Damn." He fished out his phone.

"Hi, this is Allyson, leave a message." Voice mail.

"Sweetheart, please call me. I need to know you're safe." Zeke pulled away from her apartment building and started driving.

He drove by Sweet and Savory. The parking lot was empty. He drove by her office. It was Sunday, so the lot was empty too. Zeke checked every place he could think of, but there was no sign of her blue truck.

What could he do now? He checked her apartment building once again. Nothing. He checked his phone. No messages, no text, nothing. Even though he'd called and texted. Where was she?

He hit the steering wheel. He'd messed this up. With a sigh, he drove to Wicked Sanctuary. The Dom meeting was going to start soon, and maybe they'd know what he should do.

He'd just pulled into the parking lot of Wicked Sanctuary when his phone rang. Dani's name flashed on his phone. "Dani," he said.

"Zeke, thank God." Her voice was tinged with panic.

"What's wrong, Dani?"

"I think Allyson is in trouble."

"What kind of trouble?" He was about to restart his truck when Max came over, and Zeke lowered the window. "Dani, I'm putting you on speaker with Max."

"Now tell us why you think Allyson's in trouble?" Zeke's gut clenched so hard he thought he was going to be sick.

"Allyson called me about thirty minutes ago. She was upset. We talked, and I thought she was better, but…" Her voice broke up. "Zeke, she's in Seattle."

Zeke swore.

"What does that mean?" Max asked.

"Zeke, I didn't realize until she called me and told me she'd be checking in every thirty minutes that she was going to a private party." Dani was practically sobbing.

"Dani, calm down." Max's voice was firm.

Zeke stared at him.

"Yes, Master Max."

"Good girl. Do you know where she might have gone?"

"I have a good idea."

"Good." Max looked at him. "Zeke is coming to pick you up. You will take him to where you believe Allyson is."

"Yes, Master Max. I'll be waiting for Zeke."

The line went dead. "Dani is at Sweet and Savory where the subs were all meeting today," Max said.

"The parking lot was empty when I went by there earlier." It suddenly dawned on Zeke that it was almost four. He'd been looking for Allyson for hours. "That's why I came here. To ask for advice." Zeke's mind spun at the turn of events.

"Listen Zeke, some of those private parties in Seattle are nothing more than BDSM wannabes looking for some fun. If Allyson is alone and upset, she might not be in the right frame of mind to tell someone no."

"You don't seemed shocked by all this," Zeke said.

"I'm a Dom and a club owner. I've seen a lot." Max grasped his shoulder. "Allyson is worth fighting for. No matter what made her run. Make sure she understands that."

"I'll do that."

"And if you need help, call me. A group of Doms can be there before you know it."

"Will do." Zeke was surprised by the offer. Well, maybe not. They were family at Wicked Sanctuary. His gut tightened. Family. Allyson didn't realize it, but she had a family right here.

Zeke pulled away from Max and headed to Sweet and Savory. Dani was standing outside with the subs surrounding her. They were subdued as they waved as Dani hopped into his truck and they took off.

"Tell me everything Allyson said," Zeke told Dani.

"She wasn't making a lot of sense. Something about not being good enough."

Zeke swore as he merged onto the freeway. "Where in Seattle am I going?" It was Sunday and traffic could be a bitch.

"Industrial district." She fiddled with her phone. "The place we want is at the corner of South Hudson and First Street."

"What the hell is she doing there?" He sped up.

"That's where the party is being held." Dani wrung her hands together. "I can't understand her falling back into that old pattern. She told you about the private parties she attended in Seattle, right?"

His blood ran cold. "A bit. But she indicated she was done with them."

"I thought so too. But Zeke, she sounded dejected, like her life didn't matter anymore."

"Damn it." A semi pulled into his lane going fifty-five. Zeke swung into an empty lane and sped up.

"I tried to talk her into coming to my house if nothing else, but she wouldn't listen. She kept saying she wasn't worthy, and she needed to forget. What happened?"

"We had breakfast with my parents and sister. Questions about her parents and childhood came up." Zeke still couldn't figure out why that triggered Allyson. She'd told him her parents weren't faithful to each other. Was she afraid she couldn't be faithful? "We got back to my house, were talking, and she lost it."

"Her parents. I should have guessed."

"What is the deal with her parents? She said she hasn't seen them since she was eighteen, and they weren't a part of her life."

"They were never a part of her life."

"What do you mean?" Zeke wondered about that, but whenever he brought it up, Allyson shut down. And look where that landed them. He should have sat her down and pulled the information out of her.

"It's not my story to tell." Dani sighed. "Zeke, it isn't you. Allyson doesn't understand what a true relationship is about. She was like this when she first came to live with me and my grandparents."

"What did you do?" Zeke spied the exit he needed.

"Gave her time. It helped that we're the same age and female. My grandparents gave her space to make her own mistakes."

Zeke slowed down as he turned onto South Hudson, checking the addresses. Actually, it wasn't hard to find. There were cars parked all over the place. He finally found a place to park on the side street.

"You should stay here," Zeke said as he climbed out of the truck.

"No." Dani hopped out. "If I know this one, you're going to need me to get in."

As they walked closer, the beat of the music

rattled the blacked-out windows. Zeke's muscles tightened. With the music that loud a person couldn't even hear themselves think, much less hear someone yelling a safeword.

"I need you to act like my Dom," Dani whispered as they started up the stairs.

Zeke opened his mouth when he saw movement out of the corner of his eye. He turned his head and saw Allyson being pulled around the side of the building. "This way." He grasped Dani by the arm and led her away from the door.

"Let me go!" That was Allyson's voice. Zeke didn't hesitate; he pulled Dani with him as he ran around the side of the building.

He saw Allyson struggling with a man. Zeke didn't even think; he let go of Dani and grabbed the guy by the shoulders. "She's mine."

"Hey man, she walked back here with me."

"Liar." Allyson shook her head. Her hair was a mess, but her clothing looked intact. Good thing or Zeke might have really lost his temper.

"Dani, get Allyson to the truck." Zeke, holding the man down with one arm, fought to keep his anger under control as he dug out his keys and tossed them to Dani.

Dani went to Allyson's side. "It's okay, Allyson. We're here. Let me get you to Zeke's vehicle."

"I fucking messed up. I'm so sorry." The anguish in Allyson's voice as they walked off tore at Zeke's heart. He kept the guy in his hold until Dani and Allyson were out of sight.

"Isn't one chick enough for you?" the man sneered.

"Shut the fuck up." Zeke pushed the guy away. "Be grateful she's unharmed." With that, he jogged away from the ass and to the truck.

"Where's your truck?" Zeke asked Allyson, his tone harsher than normal.

"At the train station at home." Allyson's voice was quiet.

"How the hell did you get here?"

"Ride share from the train station." She shivered in Dani's hold. Zeke took his keys from Dani and helped both women into his truck.

He grabbed a blanket he kept in the back and handed it to Dani. "Put this over Allyson. She's going into shock." As much as he wanted to be the one to comfort her, he needed to get them out of here. Plus the anger and hurt flowing through him needed to dissipate before he thought about discussing what had happened.

"I'm so sorry. That ass wouldn't listen." Her words were quiet.

"It's okay. You're safe now," Zeke said, running his fingers over her cheek. "You'll always be safe with me."

He drew in deep breath and shut the passenger door. He wanted to punch something, preferably the ass that scared Allyson. He climbed into the truck and started it.

"I..." Tears ran down Allyson cheeks.

"Fuck." Zeke hit the steering wheel. He turned to

her. "Allyson, sweetheart." Zeke placed his arm over the back of the seat. "Don't cry. You're safe. Dani and I are not going to let anyone hurt you."

She blinked at him. Almost like she wasn't seeing him. Zeke's gut clenched to the point of pain.

"I've got her," Dani said. "Drive."

Dani was right; they needed to get out of there, but Zeke felt useless, and it wasn't a feeling he liked at all. He wanted to grab Allyson and hold her close. As he drove, Dani spoke softly to Allyson. He couldn't make out the words, but her tone was soothing.

"I think she fell asleep," Dani said softly when they were ten miles from Pleasant Valley.

"Good." They hadn't gotten much sleep last night; she'd been worried about breakfast with his parents.

"If you'll take us to my apartment, she can stay with me tonight."

"I'm not leaving her, tonight or ever," Zeke said, dropping into his Dom voice to cut to the chase with Dani. He couldn't leave Allyson any more than he could cut out his own heart. He needed to be there if she needed him, if only for tonight. His emotions were all over the place. Guilt sat low in his belly, along with confusion about why she ran, relief that she was unharmed, and frustration that he was failing her and didn't have a fucking clue how.

"I get it, but please, Sir, can we go to my apartment? Not saying your place would be scary for her, but if she happens to wake, she'll be more comfortable at my apartment."

"All right. You'll have to give me directions."

Dani was right, even if he didn't agree. He wanted Allyson at his home in his bed.

Within twenty minutes, he pulled into a parking spot in Dani's apartment complex. Allyson was still asleep. Zeke picked her up and carried her inside. Her cheeks were two bright red splotches on an otherwise pale face.

His gut tightened. What if they hadn't gone to breakfast with his family today? He should have warned his family about personal questions, especially his sister. What if he hadn't found her in time outside that party? Zeke tightened his hold on Allyson, and she moaned in her sleep.

Dani opened her apartment door. Lights flared.

"Motion sensors," Dani said. "Guest bedroom is this way."

Zeke followed Dani. The bedroom was small but held a nice double bed and a dresser with a small TV on top of it. He laid Allyson on the floral sheets after Dani pulled back the covers.

"I'll get her out of her clothes. If you'd wait in the living room." Dani held up her hand when he opened his mouth. "I know you're her Dom, but if she wakes, she could panic. Do you want to risk hurting your relationship more if she thinks you're one of the Doms from the party?"

Zeke closed his eyes. Leave it to a sub to make him see the light. "I get it."

"Good. If you need a drink, in the kitchen, the cabinet on the right, glasses right next to that."

"Thanks, Dani." Zeke gave Allyson one last look

before he left the room. It was better to let Dani take care of Allyson. Even if he had to fight himself to leave the room.

He glanced at the light beige sofa with a matching loveseat arranged in an L-shape as he made his way to the kitchen. There was a good size TV across the room, and bookcases lined the wall along with some interesting art on the wall.

A whimper floated through the air, and he rushed back to the bedroom, stopping in the doorway to find Dani smoothing the hair back from Allyson's face. "It's okay, Allyson. You're safe." Dani's voice carried to where he stood. After a moment, things were quiet. With a silent curse, Zeke went into the kitchen.

Just as Dani told him, alcohol on the left. Whisky and brandy. He grabbed both bottles, two glasses, and made his way into the living room.

He sank down on the sofa and poured himself a whisky and knocked it back. He closed his eyes as it burned its way through his body. Zeke blew out a breath. Part of him wanted to drink straight from the bottle, but that wouldn't solve anything. He needed to be alert for Allyson's sake.

Dani walked out of the bedroom but left the door open a bit. She flopped down on the sofa. Zeke waved at the bottles.

"Whisky, please. Neat."

He poured Dani two generous fingers, expecting her to sip it, but she knocked it back. "Thank you, I needed that." She sighed before setting the glass on the table and resting her head against the back of the sofa.

"Allyson asleep?"

"Yes, she barely moved when I took her shoes and jeans off. What the fuck was she thinking?" Dani's cheeks turned pink when she realized what she said. "Sorry."

"Don't be. I was thinking the same thing. You said Allyson fell back into old patterns. She told me about the Seattle parties and indicated they were in her past."

"I thought they were." Dani sat up and curled her legs under her. "When I came home a little over a year ago, I went to one of the parties with her. The minute we got inside, I knew we shouldn't be there. I dragged her out of there and got her to promise never to go again. And she didn't until tonight." She sighed. "Zeke, tell me again happened today?"

Zeke explained once again.

Dani swore when he was finished, and Zeke eyebrows rose. "Why won't Allyson understand she has worth, that she's nothing like her parents?"

He was about to ask her more when his phone rang. Zeke saw Max's name and answered it. "Hey, Max. Yeah, we got Allyson, and she's fine." Physically at least. "I'm at Dani's place."

"I'm glad you got her. I'll let everyone know. The subs were quite upset."

Damn, he'd forgotten the sub meeting. "Thank you."

"No worries. If you need anything at all, let me know." The line went dead, and Zeke set his phone on the table.

"Allyson doesn't realize how she's touched everyone's lives, that they care about her," Dani said.

"What do you mean?" He wanted to hear what Dani had to say, because he and Allyson would have a future together. They needed to get past this episode to have one.

"The nights she's been at Wicked Sanctuary, she sits and talks with the subs, and they talk to her. It's been good for her and all the subs." Dani shifted. "It took her years to let her guard down with my grandparents, yet with the subs, it happened rather quickly."

"Do your grandparents know about Wicked Sanctuary?"

"I think everyone in town does after the press conference Damon and Tessa had several months ago. But if you're asking if it upsets them, it doesn't. My grandparents are laid back. They know I'm into kink and I belong to the club."

"Allyson said she lived with you and your grandparents." He wondered about that.

"Yes, for about four years. We were both attending college locally, so it didn't make sense to do the dorm thing." Dani yawned.

"Why don't you go to bed. I can sleep on the sofa."

"You don't have to stay, Zeke. I'll be fine with Allyson on my own."

"I know you would be." He wasn't about to leave, not tonight. "I need to be here for my own piece of mind. To make sure she's okay."

"I get it." Dani stood up. "I'll get you a pillow and blanket." Dani walked out of the room and returned a few minutes later. "The bedrooms share a bathroom, and there's another bathroom on the other side of the kitchen."

"Thank you." He took the bed things from her. "I'll take care of those," he said as she reached for the bottles and glasses. "Go get some rest, Dani. If you need me, I'm here."

Dani nodded and walked into her bedroom, closing the door after her. Zeke set the blanket and pillow on the sofa before he picked up the bottles and glasses and took them into the kitchen.

He quietly washed up the two glasses before he went back into the living room. Zeke picked up his phone. It was barely eight, yet it felt like midnight. He checked his emails and answered a text from Gabriel.

A noise came from the room Allyson was in. Setting his phone down, Zeke crept to the room where Allyson slept. A whimper reached his ears.

He pushed the door open slowly. Dani had left a small lamp on. Allyson whimpered again as she twisted on the bed. Zeke crept closer. He didn't want to scare her, but he wanted her to know she wasn't alone, and she was safe.

"Allyson, sweetheart," he whispered.

"No, please. I said no." Her voice was soft as she fought with the covers.

His gut clenched. What had that bastard done before he got there? Zeke stopped next to the bed.

"Zeke, I'm sorry. Come find me, please." The pleading note in her voice broke him. He sat and ran his fingers over her cheek.

"I'm here, sweetheart. You're safe."

"Zeke?" Her eyes were closed, but she stopped thrashing.

He didn't hesitate. He kicked off his shoes and positioned himself so he could pull Allyson into his arms. "Yes, sweetheart. I'm here; you're safe."

She trembled in his hold. "Oh, Zeke, I'm so sorry. I messed up."

"Shhhhh." He ran his palm over her hair in a soothing motion. "We'll talk later. Just rest. I'll keep you safe. No one will hurt you."

Her breathing evened out, and her body relaxed against his. Zeke shifted into a more comfortable position on the small bed. Allyson needed him. He'd sleep on a bed of nails for her.

Not that he planned on sleeping. He had a lot of things to think about. One was how to get past Allyson's childhood issues and why she felt she had no self-worth. If she couldn't get past that, there might not be a future for them at all.

Chapter 11

Allyson shifted. She didn't want to wake up. Memories flooded her, and she cringed inwardly at what might have happened. She was afraid to find out where she was—or wasn't. Wait a second… Memories of Zeke telling her she was safe filtered in. Gathering her courage, she opened her eyes.

She was lying on a male chest. Tension filled her. Allyson tilted her head, and all the tension left her body when she saw Zeke's face, both grateful she was safe and scared to death that she'd screwed up the one good thing in her life.

"Good morning." Zeke's voice was rough.

"Ah, good morning." His eyes were soft from slumber and his face relaxed. That was a good sign, right?

The bedroom door creaked open. "I heard voices," Dani's cheery voice made Allyson smile.

"We're awake," Zeke said.

"Good. I've got coffee brewing."

"Thanks, Dani," Zeke said as he gazed down at Allyson.

"We're at Dani's place?"

"Yes." He sat up, and she maneuvered away from

his warm body. Instantly, she missed his arms around her. "What time it is?"

"Eight-thirty," Dani said, poking her head back in the room. "Zeke, your phone is vibrating off the table."

He groaned. "Yeah, I bet."

"I'm late for work." Allyson started to scramble out of bed.

"Take it easy," Dani said. "I called your boss and explained you were too sick to call in."

Allyson glanced down at the floor. Damn, now Dani was lying to her boss for her. "Thanks, Dani." Oh hell, she was in her underwear. Zeke had seen her in less, though right now, she felt more vulnerable than she ever had. She was sure she'd lost any chance of Zeke sticking around. This time, instead of being unwanted, she'd pushed him away. Allyson wanted to curl into a ball and cry.

"No problem." Dani backed out of the room.

Zeke tipped her head up with his finger. "It's all right, honey. We have to talk, but for now, we need to breathe. Both of us."

Was he throwing her a safety net until she could put last night well behind her, or did he mean it? Zeke had never hedged with her before. She looked into his eyes, saw the honesty there, and nodded. It didn't mean he wasn't leaving her, but a thread of hope settled into her heart, and Allyson clung to it like a lifeline.

"Good girl. I'll use the bathroom off the kitchen and check who is texting me. Meet you in the kitchen."

Before she could say anything, he walked out of the room. Was he angry? She didn't think so, but then what did she know? She'd fucked this up royally by going to the party yesterday.

She'd warned Zeke she was bad at relationships. *Oh grow up, Young. You're the one who messed this up.* She couldn't argue with that voice inside her. Now to explain things to Zeke.

A sigh escaped her lips as she walked into the bathroom. Dani left her freshly cleaned jeans and shirt on the counter. There was a package of underwear in her size with a note. "Bought these a while back, take them. D."

Stripping, Allyson hopped in the shower. Twenty minutes later, she stood in the doorway of the kitchen watching Dani and Zeke together. They could make a cute couple. Allyson's lips turned up. Dani had a thing for Gabriel, Zeke's business partner, so she had no worries there. Other worries killed the smile though. There was a lot to sort out, and right now, all she could do was pray that Zeke would listen to her and give her a chance since she messed things up so badly.

"Good morning, again," Allyson said, a little too brightly.

"Morning." Dani stood and went to the counter to pour a cup of coffee and held it out to Allyson. "I'll let you add what you want. You know I can never get it right for you."

"Thanks." She added some cream and sugar. Lots

of sugar.

"Someone has a sweet tooth," Zeke said.

"In coffee yes." She stirred her coffee, then carried it over to the table and sat down. "I want to apologize to both of you."

"For what?" Dani asked, sitting down.

"Last night. I acted rashly." She looked down at the table.

"You did," Zeke remarked, and her head jerked up. She didn't expect him to agree with her.

"Zeke—" Dani started, but he held up his hand, and she fell silent.

"It was reckless."

Allyson sucked in a breath. Zeke was right. It had been reckless and more. Dani shifted in her seat.

"Umm, I think I'll run to the bakery and get us some breakfast." Dani all but ran out of the kitchen.

"You're right," Allyson told Zeke softly.

"I don't understand why you did it. I'm just glad you called Dani." Zeke splayed his hands on the table. "We can't move forward until we recover from this, Allyson. And that means some truth from you."

Her heart stopped. "I…" Allyson closed her eyes and tried to breathe.

"We're a couple. We're supposed to work out these problems out together, but you raced off without giving me a chance."

"We are a couple. I hope."

Stark pain etched lines in Zeke's face. Oh Lord, what had she done?

"Couples don't run out on each other." He tapped

his fingers on the table. "What's going on? What sent you to Seattle?"

Allyson clutched her coffee cup tight. He'd never understand how different his family was from hers. How she'd never known the love he had, and she wasn't sure she was capable of that kind of love. She couldn't even think about how to begin.

Zeke stood suddenly. "I guess that's my answer. You're not ready to talk. When you are, you know where to find me."

"Zeke." She could barely get his name out as tears clogged her throat.

"Don't take too long, Allyson." With that, he walked out of Dani's apartment.

Allyson sat there, stunned, with tears running down her cheeks. What had she done? She'd lost the only man she'd ever loved because she panicked. Oh, my God. She did love him. She'd never thought herself capable of loving, of being loved, and now she'd lost any chance. What was she going to do?

Folding her arms on the table, she laid her head on them and cried. Her body shook with her sobs. Could she get Zeke back?

* * * *

Every step Zeke took away from Dani's apartment cut into his heart like glass. He loved Allyson. It wasn't such a shock as it had been last night. He loved her so much, but he wouldn't watch her go down a path of self-destruction. The hurt ran deep that she couldn't confide in him, couldn't help him to understand what had happened.

If she was going to run every time someone asked about her parents or her childhood, then what kind of relationship could they have? Not a good one.

His phone beeped. Gabriel. Zeke texted Gabriel that he was on his way home. Gabriel would have to handle things today because he couldn't.

Zeke climbed into his truck and sat there for several minutes before starting it and driving away. He had no idea what was going to happen next or how he'd be able to deal with Allyson in a professional capacity. But for today, he was going to wallow in self-pity and self-reflection. Because, right now, he hurt too much to think about the future or his work.

* * * *

Two days later, Zeke came home to see Allyson sitting on his front porch. Two incredibly long, fucked up days that he could barely remember. After two days of silence, he figured she'd made her choice, and he'd never see her again. He parked his truck and climbed out. By the time he reached the stairs, she was standing near the front door.

"Hi, Zeke. Can we talk?" Her voice was tentative.

"Sure." He opened the front door and waved her in. There were shadows under her eyes that he wanted to soothe. Instead, he stuck his hands in his pockets and led her into the family room, not caring about shoes or floors or anything. She sat down in one of the chairs, and he took one across from her.

"Do you want something to drink?" he asked. His mother would kick his ass if he didn't at least offer her a beverage.

"No, thank you."

So polite. Zeke sat back and waited. The last few days had been hell on him. He'd called Gabriel and told him he was taking a few days off, which had been a mistake. It gave him too much time to think.

Gabriel was surprised but understood. Today, Zeke had to get out of his house. He'd gone for a long drive and ended up at Wicked Sanctuary. Max found him sitting in the parking lot and got him to come inside.

They talked about everything and anything but Allyson. It gave Zeke a sense of normalcy, and on the drive home, he decided it was time for him to get his ass back to work.

While he'd left her on Monday with an ultimatum, he'd been thinking he'd been too tough on her. She'd told him about her parents' infidelity, which had left scars on her, but he wasn't sure how to get her to understand he wasn't like that. Lord, he hoped she wasn't here to tell him it was over. That she couldn't be with him. He fought against the pain coursing through his body.

The silence between them continued, and Zeke shifted in his seat. "Why are you here, Allyson?"

"To apologize."

"If that's all," he started to stand. His entire body hurt, but not more than his heart.

"There's more." Her voice was soft, but a thread of regret flowed from it.

"Oh?"

"You are not making this easy." Her blue eyes were clouded with doubt.

"It's not my job to make it easy. My job is to help you work through any issues, except you won't let me. But it is also important for me to keep you safe, and I failed."

"What?"

* * * *

Allyson sat up straight. "Zeke, you didn't fail." How could he think that? "I'm the one who messed up. Big time."

Zeke stared at her with those knowing eyes of his. She had to make this right, even if they had nothing beyond a professional relationship after this. A dagger pierced her heart at the thought, but she had to do this. She'd thought long and hard over the past couple days and nights.

She'd barely slept, but today she made the decision to tell Zeke everything. If he still wanted her, then they'd figure it out. If not, so be it. She'd turn his jobs over to another inspector once they had someone up to speed.

But she couldn't give up the Wicked Sanctuary job. Max had already insisted that no matter what happened between her and Zeke, she was staying on that job. Allyson had almost laughed at the Dom tone in Max's voice, but she couldn't. Not yet.

"I failed you." Allyson twisted her hands together in her lap.

"What scared you so much you ran to a play party? I want to understand."

"I know you do." Allyson sat for a moment. When she'd practiced this in her head, it seemed so simple, but now her emotions were all over the place. Her love for this man in front of her. Her pain that she'd hurt him. "I told you a little bit about my parents."

"You said they weren't faithful to each other."

"It was more than that." She took a deep breath. "Zeke, my parents were swingers."

He blinked at her, then his eyes widened.

"I don't share that with a lot of people."

He nodded. "But why did that make you run? Did you think I wouldn't understand?"

"You've always been part of a loving family, as Dani has." Allyson inhaled and met his gaze head on. "I never had that in my life. From the time I was little, there were parties. I was left a lot of times to fend for myself. I learned to eat dry cereal because I couldn't lift the milk out of the fridge."

"Fuck."

"Yeah. My parents cared more about partying than they did about me." Her belly tumbled with her words. "I was lucky they got me into school, but I was the one who got myself up every morning, got dressed, got to school."

"Didn't you tell anyone?"

She shook her head. "I was too young to understand, but as I got older, I was ashamed of my parents' actions. There were rumors, and sometimes kids were nasty to me, but once I left home, and my parents moved away, I thought all my fears went away."

"You grew up here in Pleasant Valley?"

"Yes. We lived by the wetlands, in a rundown house near the trailer park." She laughed. "I might not be trailer trash, but I'm close."

"Like hell you are." His brown eyes turned fierce. "You are a woman of worth, and don't let anyone tell you you're not."

"Too late. I've struggled with that my entire life, never feeling worthy of love."

He opened his mouth, but she forestalled him with a hand in the air.

"Until Dani and her grandparents, I'd never even known affection. I felt invisible. I can't tell you how many times I yearned for someone, anyone to show they noticed me. I think that's why I started going to those parties. To be noticed."

Zeke's hands clutched the sides of his chair as if he wanted to jump up. But he kept quiet.

"By the time I met you, I'd pretty much decided going solo would be my life. Especially since, not only was I not loved, but if anyone ever found out about my parents…"

"No one worth anything is going to hold your parents' choices against you," he ground out.

Allyson laughed, and even she heard the bitterness in it. "Come on, Zeke. People who don't understand the lifestyle wouldn't get what my parents did. You come from a loving family, a family that obviously cares about you. I have no family."

"But you do have family." Zeke leaned forward. "You have Dani, me, everyone at Wicked Sanctuary.

Allyson, you have a family of the heart."

"It's taken me a long time to realize that." Her breath hiccupped. "I hate my parents because they neglected me. I couldn't figure out why they couldn't love me." Her breathing was choppy. "Is it too late? For us?"

"Why did you run?"

"I was scared."

"Of me?"

"Not you, but your family." She spread her hands out in front of her. "Zeke, I've never known a family like yours. You care about each other. When Josie started asking more and more about my childhood, I realized I was drowning. If they found out, I'd never be able to live with the looks in their faces. The pity in their eyes would have destroyed me."

"I'm sorry Josie did that. I did speak with her about it."

"But you shouldn't have to."

"It's none of their business."

"Maybe."

"No maybe about it." He reached out and captured her hand in his.

"The second I walked up the stairs to go into the party, I knew I'd made a mistake." He squeezed her hand. "I sat on the steps for a bit, working things out in my head, I'd just gotten up to check in with Dani when that guy grabbed me."

Zeke's hands tightened on hers.

"I told him no; I screamed no. I fought, but he was stronger. But I wasn't about to let anything happen."

"How would you stop him?"

"Mace." She gave a small smile. "I carry a can with me when I go to the parties."

"Smart girl."

"Yeah, well, you arrived and saved me. So you see, you're not a failure."

"I will always save you."

Her heart swelled, and for the first time, Allyson felt hope. "I've never known the kind of love your family has. I know Dani's grandparents love her, but I never had that. My parents ignored me my entire life."

"I'm sorry for that. Someone should have called child services."

"I don't think anyone realized, but as I got older, it got worse." A shiver traveled up her spine.

"What do you mean?"

"Once I was older, I realized that they didn't care about me at all. It was always about them. You know, I tried to get a job when I was sixteen but couldn't because I had to have parental consent. I couldn't even get them to sign the damn form."

"Oh baby. I hate that you were all alone."

"I wasn't completely. I suspect Dani's grandparents knew what was going on, but they had no idea how to approach me about it. Her grandmother made sure I ate dinner with them almost every night, and I spent weekends with Dani."

"They protected you."

"I guess."

"Are your parents still in Montana?"

"Yes. They're living in some swinger commune there. It's their life, and I leave them to it."

"But they had a responsibility to you. It's amazing that you're even into the kink lifestyle after all that."

Allyson grinned. "Well, kink wasn't what drew me to the parties. I'm kind of ashamed to say this, but I thought that's how most people lived. The parties and multiple partners."

"Of course you did. You had no real examples in your life, except maybe Dani's grandparents."

"True. But, honestly, it started to feel wrong a few years ago. So I stopped going pretty much. The last one I went to before this last weekend was with Dani right after she came home from San Francisco last year. She made me promise not to go anymore"

"Then I started to pursue you?"

"Kind of. I had stopped going when you asked me out the first time."

"You said you'd been in a relationship, but that was the first time I asked you out. What about the second time?"

"I wasn't in the right head space. I guess I never was." She shifted. "But after that day in the bookstore, we connected."

"I thought we did."

"I'm so sorry I hurt you like I did, Zeke. I panicked and fell back onto something I thought to be true. But it wasn't. I was lying to myself. It was a crutch I used to avoid relationships. I see that now."

"What does that mean for us?"

Allyson closed her eyes and opened them. "I hope

you'll give me another chance." Zeke released her hands, and her heart clenched. "I never thanked you for holding me Sunday night after I had my nightmare."

"Sweetheart." He stood up and started pacing. "I don't know what to say right now."

"You don't have to say anything. I'm the one who screwed us up. Our relationship was good until I stopped trusting you. I'm so sorry, Zeke. Maybe I should go?" Allyson wasn't sure how much longer she could sit here without breaking down. She stood.

"No." Zeke turned to her. "Please, Allyson, sit back down and let me gather my thoughts."

Allyson retook her seat and waited while Zeke paced around the room. This was what she'd done to him, and she owed him his chance to have a say, good or bad. Her heart stuttered. Lord, she loved this man.

Her breath caught in her throat. She did love him. The relationship she'd been running from was right there in front of her. Zeke had shown her in a thousand ways how special she was, and maybe it was time she believed him.

"First things first," Zeke started as he turned to face her. The pain etched in his features froze her in her seat. "I think I understand why you panicked. My family can be overwhelming." He glanced out the back patio doors, then back to her. "I can't go through what happened on Sunday ever again."

"I understand." This time when she stood, he kept silent. "I'm sorry I screwed us up." Allyson moved toward the front door.

A warm hand captured her arm. She looked up to see Zeke staring down at her with determination and something else shining in his eyes. "I need assurances from you that you won't take off half-cocked when you panic." He pulled her to him. "I will always be there when you need me. All you have to do is tell me what the issue is. Just trust me."

Tears filled her eyes. "I do, Zeke. I lost sight of that for a moment, but I trust you more than I've ever trusted anyone."

"Good. You need to remember that. Always. And always use your safe word if you're uncomfortable, but tell me why. I deserve that much."

She nodded. "And so much more."

Zeke drew in a deep breath. Here it comes, she thought. The gentle "I can't do this anymore" that would seal her fate. She had to be strong, to let him say the words. It would help him to heal, something that might never happen for her. But she owed him this, so she kept her gaze on him, shoring up her own strength with the kindness in his eyes. She would hold it together until later. She had to, for Zeke.

"Listen, I don't want to panic or scare you further, but I have to say this. I love you."

She froze in his embrace. Fresh tears sprang to her eyes. "Oh Zeke." She hadn't expected this. "I love you too. I'm sorry I ran; I won't do it again." Tears trailed down her cheeks.

"Sweetheart." He pulled her close. "Don't cry."

"I can't help it. I don't deserve you."

"You do. You deserve someone who loves you

and is willing to put the work in to prove he's trustworthy." He cradled her against his warm chest.

"I might need to hear that every day of my life."

"I'll make sure I say that along with I love you. Loving you is easy; having a relationship is hard, but we'll get through this together."

More tears fell. "Together."

Epilogue

Allyson smiled at Zeke as he walked toward her at Wicked Sanctuary. Three weeks had passed since they made up. And what a make-up it had been. A little bit of discipline and a lot of loving. She still warmed thinking about it.

Two weeks since she started talking with a kink-friendly psychologist. It would take a lot longer than two weeks to fix what she experienced in her childhood, but now she was learning about her reactions and how to control them. And how to ask for help.

She had been so happy in these few weeks. They'd gone to breakfast with his parents again, including his sister. Before that, Zeke, with her permission, had a frank talk with his family, explaining that her parents and childhood were off limits until she was ready to share.

Josie apologized for her previous questioning, and Allyson teased her she should be a lawyer rather than a doctor. Josie hadn't meant to pry or upset Allyson; she was being protective of her older brother.

In a way, Allyson understood — or was beginning to. She glanced around the club. Zeke was right. She had a family here. A family that understood her fears and were all willing to help her no matter what she needed.

"I love you," the words were whispered in her ear.

"I love you, too, Sir." She turned her head and kissed his cheek. "Done?"

"Yes. Max told me to take the rest of the night off."

"That was nice of him."

"I think it was more because I couldn't keep my eyes off of you."

"Why? I'm not wearing anything different." She was wearing a halter-top and boy shorts.

"Because I can't wait to get you home."

"Ah." A smile curved her lips. "Why don't you tie me up here tonight?"

His eyes widened, then he came around to face her. "In the club?"

"That's where we are." She'd come to this decision while talking to her doctor. She needed to give Zeke something special, and her submission in the club would be the first step.

"Sweetheart, are you sure?"

"I am. I've heard people talking about how they want to see your Shibari. So let's give them a show tonight."

His eyes lit up. "You are... I don't know what to say."

"I trust and love you. No one here will think me odd or slutty because I want you to do this. I want to give you this gift."

"It's a gift I humbly accept." He pulled her to her feet. "And when we get home tonight, I'm going to possess you in every other way."

"I wouldn't want it any other way."

* * * *

Thank you for reading *Possess,* the fifth book in the Wicked Sanctuary series. If you enjoyed this book, please consider leaving a review on Amazon, Goodreads, or wherever you prefer, and know that it would be greatly appreciated.

For new release information and news about Marie Tuhart, please join her newsletter.

If you enjoyed *Possess, Tantalize* will be released in spring of 2022.

ABOUT THE AUTHOR

Marie Tuhart lives in the beautiful Pacific Northwest. She loves to read and write, and when she's not writing, she spends time with her two dogs, Tommy and Trina, family, traveling and enjoying life.

Marie is a multi-published author with The Wild Rose Press and Trifecta Publishing, and is self-published. To be alerted to her new releases, you can join Marie's newsletter or check out her website: **www.mairetuhart.com**

OTHER BOOKS BY MARIE TUHART

PREVIEW OF *TANTALIZE*

Dani Wright secured her long black hair into a ponytail and then slipped on the pink and white wristband. She made sure all her other belongings were in the locker before she shut the door and secured it. Dani was smiling when she walked out to the front desk.

"Evening, Ralph."

Ralph turned and grinned at her. "Hey Dani. We've got a full house tonight since it's the Fourth of July party."

Dani sat down on the wooden chair. "I figured as much. Wicked Sanctuary parties are always well attended."

"That they are."

She logged into the computer and began to get her station ready. The doors would open in about ten minutes.

"I'd like to try something different tonight," Ralph said. "I'll check people in and then they can sign in with you and go on their way. This way, maybe the line will move faster."

"Whatever works for you."

Dani took a deep breath. She'd been living in a furnished place as temporary measure and had finally found an apartment she wanted to move into. She'd signed the lease before she came out to Wicked Sanctuary tonight, and the apartment manager told her she could move in right away.

Most of her stuff was in storage, and it wasn't like she had that much. She had sold everything when she left San Francisco. Most of what was in storage was personal stuff that she didn't have room for where she was living.

Ralph stood up and unlocked the door and then took his seat it was barely a minute later before the door opened and people started coming in oh yes tonight was going to be busy. Good it would keep her mind off of everything she needed to do this weekend.

* * * *

Gabriel Quinn stepped out of his SUV and shut the door. It was a good thing Max was expanding the parking lot along with the club; it was packed tonight. Of course Gabriel expected that with it being a members only party.

He sauntered towards the front door, not surprised to see a small line, but it seemed to be moving quickly. Gabriel didn't care. He hadn't been very interested in playing lately and he knew why.

Dani.

He'd found out a couple months ago, at the opening of the bookstore attached to Kleinman's, that she was home, and ever since, his mind had been preoccupied with her. Dani could always tie him in knots, and even though she'd been gone several years, seeing her again was no different.

Not that he hadn't dated in the years she was gone. Heck, he'd even played with a couple of the club subs, but now that Dani was back, he found he was still interested in her. But they weren't completely compatible. When he tried to introduce her to kink when they were in college together, she'd freaked out.

He wouldn't go through that again. No, it was better this way. Maybe he'd give himself a break and stay away from the club for a while. Get his head straightened out about Dani and what her being back meant.

He stepped in front of Ralph's station and smiled. "Good evening," Ralph said. "I've got you checked in. Sign in at the next station, and you'll be all set to go."

Gabriel nodded and stepped in front of the next station. The woman behind the computer glanced up. "Dani?" *What the hell was she doing in the club?*

"Hello, Sir, if you would please sign in, you can be on your way."

Her voice was calm and steady. Gabriel signed his name on the pad as directed, but he was still confused as to why she was there. "What are you doing here?"

"Working, Sir."

Gabriel opened his mouth but Ralph interrupted. "Is there a problem?"

"I don't believe so," Dani said. "You're all set. You can go into the club now."

Gabriel didn't move. He couldn't. Dani shouldn't be here.

"Let's go, Gabriel," Max said as he took Gabriel by the arm and guided him away from Dani.

Gabriel was still trying to wrap his head around Dani being there and attempt to put up a protest as

Max led him away. Something wasn't right here. Max took Gabriel into his office. He pushed the door slightly closed but not all the way.

"I take it you're surprised to see Dani here," Max said, staring at him.

"To say the very least," Gabriel said, matching Max's stare. "How long has she been a member?"

"Right after she returned home." Max continued to stare at him. "I hope this won't be an issue?"

"Damn right it's an issue." Gabriel paced around Max in the confines of his office. "Dani doesn't belong here. Kink is not her thing."